DE...
on you

One night changed everything.

JESSICA AIKEN-HALL

Depending On You

JESSICA AIKEN-HALL

MOONLIT MADNESS
PRESS

Copyright © 2022 Jessica Aiken-Hall

First Edition.

All rights reserved. No part of this publication may be reproduced, stored in any retrieval system, or transmitted, in any form or by any means, electronic, mechanical, photocopying, recording or otherwise, without the prior written permission of the author. If you would like permission to use material from the book (other than for review purposes), please contact http://jessicaaikenhall.com/contact

This is a work of fiction. Names, characters, businesses, organizations, products, places, and events portrayed in this novel are either products of the author's imagination or used fictitiously. Any resemblance to actual persons, living or dead, events or locales is entirely coincidental.

ISBN-13: 978-1-955071-07-9(paper)

Library of Congress Control Number: 2021925901

Moonlit Madness Press

Cover Design © Shower of Schmidt's Design

Editor: Proofreading By the Page

For my husband, George.

Also by Jessica Aiken-Hall

Demi: Crystal River Book One

Isabelle: Crystal River Book Two

Delaney: Crystal River Book Three

Boundaries: Scope of Practice Book One

Confidentiality: Scope of Practice Book Two

Accountability: Scope of Practice Book Three

Rebecca Remains: Shadow of a Doubt Book One

Murder at Honeybee Lake: Shadow of a Doubt Book Two

House in the Woods

Reclaim Your Power: Heal Trauma by Telling Your Story

The Monster That Ate My Mommy- A Memoir

Summer
of
2018

Chapter One

CATE

Rain blew in through the open window. It was the only thing keeping me awake. Five hours on the road, with another three to go. If it wasn't for the adrenaline, I'm not sure I'd be able to make this trip. Four lanes of traffic were far more than I could stand. The only saving grace was it was three A.M. The silver lining.

I leaned into the headrest and laughed. "Oh, Patti, you're always in my head." The smile on my face disappeared as quickly as it had arrived when the reason for my impromptu road trip blasted across the radio. I reached over to turn it off. My heart shot into my throat as my knuckles turned white on the steering wheel.

The past twenty years had flown by. Except the memories still haunted me. I knew it would only be a matter of time before I'd have to pay for what we did. What I did. I've got to make it to Patti before she hears the news. We've always worked best together. If only I'd have moved to New Jersey when she asked. Although, distance wouldn't be able to save me, just like time wasn't.

JESSICA AIKEN-HALL

That night plays on rewind in my mind whenever it's quiet. When something goes right in my life, it soon fades away as memories pull me back to 1998. A couple of deep breaths were usually all I needed to get myself back together. But this time, I knew it was going to be different. This time I needed Patti.

I slid the mixed CD she sent me for my twentieth birthday in and let the music take me back to happier times. *Mary Jane's Last Dance* lulled me back to a simpler time when we still had our innocence. With the music filling my soul, there was no room for the fear. I'd get through this. I had to.

I haven't seen Patti since she came home for her mom's funeral five years ago. The vow we made to never let too much time pass between visits kept getting tested. Every visit was separated by more time. Monthly visits turned to yearly, and soon stopped happening altogether. Being together was too painful. At least, that's how it seemed, or maybe it was only that way for me.

As much as I hate to admit it, what happened that night changed us. And our friendship. How could it not? There are some things you can never overcome. No matter how tight of a bond you had before. Secrets change everything. They are toxic, bringing negativity with them everywhere you go, sticking to you like glue.

Patti seemed to shake it off better than me. Maybe that's why she never wants to talk about it, and why she's been pushing me away. Together forever. That was our blood sister's pledge. If we'd have used real blood and not just ketchup, maybe it would have been cemented. The New Radicals were right. You get what you give. I flipped to the next song. Tracy Chapman's voice was all it took to make the tears fall. This was

2

our song. The one that gave us hope of better days, and the one we'd sing when my mom started drinking. Again.

All we needed was a fast car. Ironically, what we needed would be what stole our freedom. At least mine.

Chapter Two

PATTI

In a puddle of sweat, the beating of my heart pulled me out of the reoccurring nightmare. The one I've had for the past twenty years. I reached my hand out, looking for Danny, but he wasn't there. I rolled over to his side of the bed and nuzzled my face into his pillow, inhaling his familiar scent.

Remnants of the dream twisted with the reality of what happened. After all these years, I'm not even sure anymore. I've never been able to tell where the truth ended and the lies began. And so was my life.

Visions of Cate and me, carelessly enjoying summer days together, brought emotion to the surface. I miss how it used to be. I miss her. Had it really been five years since we'd seen each other? I rolled over and watched the ceiling fan spin. What made her stay away? Or, the real question, what kept me from going home?

I knew the answer to both questions, but I didn't know how to fix it. Running away was always easiest for me. Avoidance fixed nothing, though. It just added to the problem, usually creating new ones. Like straining the most important

4

DEPENDING ON YOU

relationship I've ever had. Sure, I loved my husband, but it wasn't the same. There's just something about sisterhood. Blood or not.

The journal my therapist suggested I get to write my dreams in caught my attention. All the pages still blank. There was no way I wanted to relive such horrific events while I'm awake. The thoughts have become more persistent now. Not wanting to think about them has stopped being an option. Visions crept in. I never know when I'm going to be back in that cemetery, watching as my life was stolen from me. And there's nothing I can do about. There wasn't then, either.

Sleep was out of the question now, even with hours before my alarm plays its annoying tune. Wrapped in my pink, plush robe, I pulled it tight as I looked around the dark room. Something didn't feel right. I couldn't put my finger on it, but an uneasy feeling lingered deep within me. I placed my hand over my heart and closed my eyes. Cate needed me.

Chapter Three

CATE

My hand shook as I lifted it to knock. Three solid wraps on the mahogany door were all it took before the younger version of Patti stood before me. "Hi, I don't know if you remember me, but I'm..."

"Mom's friend, where I got my stupid name." Katie looked down at her phone and snickered.

"Nice to see you, too, Katie. Can I come in?" I took a step forward.

"She's not here." Her eyes still fixated on the screen. "She's at work."

"Where's that?" I looked around the yard behind me hoping for a clue.

"The library." Katie rolled her eyes. "Do you guys even talk anymore?"

My cheeks flushed as I twisted the jade ring on my finger. "Not as much as we should. Are you sure she's at work? Isn't that her car?" I pointed to the minivan I parked behind.

Katie poked her head past mine. "Huh? Maybe she is." She turned her head and hollered, "Mom!"

DEPENDING ON YOU

Patti strolled into the living room wearing a fluffy pink robe. "What's the matter with you now?"

Katie shook her head and walked past her mother. "You have company."

"Cate?" Patti covered her mouth.

"Hey, can I come in?" The tears began to fall before she answered. "I'm in trouble."

Patti met me on the doorstep and wrapped me in her arms. "Oh Cate. I knew something was up."

I leaned into her and sobbed. She held me tighter as my body heaved. "I don't know what I'm going to do."

"We'll get through whatever it is together. Just like we always do." Patti smoothed my hair. "Come on, let's get inside so we can talk."

I followed Patti into the kitchen where she took out two mugs and filled them with coffee. I watched her every move and thought about all the time we had lost together. "Patti, I don't know if I'm going to make it."

She turned around with the mugs in each hand. "Sit down and let's talk." She set the cups onto the table and pulled out a chair for me. "Here, have a seat."

I looked around the room. "I don't know if that's a good idea. This isn't something I want everyone to hear." I steadied myself on the table.

"Katie's the only one home right now and I can guarantee she won't hear a word we're saying." Patti smiled. "You're safe here." She put her hand on my back and guided me to the chair.

I sat down and sat on my hands as my foot tapped. "I'm terrified, Patti. I don't want to go to jail."

"What are you talking about?" She leaned forward with her elbows on the table.

7

JESSICA AIKEN-HALL

"They're opening the case back up. They're going to know what I did." I squeezed my eyes closed. "I can't go to jail. Not now, Dad needs me."

"You're not going to jail. They're not going to find anything, just like they didn't back then." Patti took a sip of coffee. Before setting the cup down she tilted her head. "What do you mean your dad needs you?"

"He's at home on hospice. I should be there with him now, but I had to come see you."

"What's wrong with him?" Patti set her mug down and leaned her head back. "You should have called me. I could have come to you."

"I didn't want to bother you with this again." I rubbed my forehead. "Sammy won't be able to handle it if I'm gone."

"Is she with him right now?" Patti turned her head to look at the clock. "We can get back there by dinner time if we leave now."

I shook my head. "No, you don't have to come. I can take care of it."

Patti stood up and tied her robe. "No, I'm going with you. I just need to let Danny know. It's not like anyone will miss me here." She picked up her phone. "I'll be right back. Go use the bathroom if you have to so we can leave as soon as I'm packed." I tried not to listen to their conversation, but as Patti's voice became louder it was hard not to.

I stood up and stretched, releasing some of the tension I had been holding onto since hearing the news. The refrigerator was covered in photos of Patti and her family. Happy, smiling faces looking back at me. I was grateful I hadn't destroyed everything for her. Under one of the photos was a picture of Patti and me.

8

DEPENDING ON YOU

I took it off and rubbed my finger over our faces. It had been a long time since I had seen those girls. Carefree and full of possibilities. It was before everything changed. Before I lost myself and my best friend. In an instant it was all taken away.

"Are you ready to go?" Patti had a duffle bag on her shoulder and a suitcase in her hand.

"Are you sure you should come? It sounds like you should stay here." I focused my attention back to the picture.

"Yeah, it's fine." She waved her hand in the air. "It's not like he's ever home."

I held the photo out for her to see. "I miss these girls."

She smiled. "Me, too. Let's change that."

I returned the photo. "How? I'm all washed up."

"That's far from true. You're beautiful now, just like you were then." Patti handed me one of her bags. "Here, help an old lady out."

"You can't say those nice things about me and then call yourself an old lady. It doesn't work like that. If I'm supposed to believe I'm beautiful, then you have to, too."

"Fine." Patti rolled her eyes and laughed. "But have you seen this ass? It's huge." She slapped her butt."

"Knock it off, you're beautiful."

"Tell that to my husband." She took a box of granola bars off the counter and turned off the kitchen light. "So, speaking of you being fine as hell, have you heard from...?"

"No. I don't have time for that in my life right now. Or ever. Besides, he's married." I followed Patti to the door.

"Oh no he's not." She bobbed her head. "Him and Cassandra got divorced."

"Really? How do you know that?"

9

"Facebook. We've kept in touch over the years. They never had any kids. I knew he didn't love her. He's always had his heart set on you."

"You're insane. It's been decades. I'm sure he's over me." I opened my trunk and put Patti's bag inside.

"That's not what he said." She shrugged. "He loved you. He asks about you every time we talk. Has he reached out to you?"

"I'm not on Facebook. I don't have enough time for my own drama, let alone everyone else's."

"Hmm, maybe you are an old lady." She grinned. "Do you want me to drive? I know how much you love it."

I tossed my keys to her. "Maybe being an old lady isn't such a bad thing if it comes with a chauffeur."

"I can get us there in six hours. Give or take a little." Patti got in and adjusted the seat.

"Will we arrive alive?" I fastened my seatbelt.

"Only time will tell." She laughed. "Yes, of course. I know some tricks to avoid some of the traffic. We'll be fine."

"Should you make sure Katie and Logan are okay before we go?"

"They're fine. They both drive now, so they're never home anyway. It's a miracle Katie was home this morning." Patti backed out of the driveway. "I don't blame them. I wouldn't want to be home, either."

"What do you mean?" I kicked the bags of trash out from under my feet.

"Danny and I haven't been getting along lately. I guess there's been some yelling." She straightened the wheel and slid on her sunglasses. "It's what happens when you're married for as long as we have been."

DEPENDING ON YOU

"No, I don't think that's how it works." I looked out the window regretting I had added my two cents. "But I wouldn't know."

"Yeah, married life isn't all it's cracked up to be. At least it's not what I had expected. You were the smart one. Single and free. Must be nice." She turned and smiled.

"Oh, yeah, it's a blast. You should envy me. I get to live at home with my dying father and annoying little sister."

"When did you move back home?" Patti glanced over the top of her sunglasses at me.

"I lost my job and my apartment soon after. I never planned on sticking around Lawrenceville, but then Dad got sick and then..."

"Where were you going to go? I never thought you wanted to leave town. That's why you didn't move to New Jersey with me."

"I don't think I'd last in a place like this. Everyone is on top of each other, and I can't stand the traffic. I'd have to walk everywhere. Or be in a constant state of panic."

"It grows on you." Patti shrugged. "Let's listen to some music. What do you have in here?"

I turned on the stereo. "Sound familiar?"

"Oh my god, I can't believe you still have this." She reached over and turned up the volume and started singing along.

"I'm surprised it still works. I listen to it when I'm missing you. Which is all the time."

"I should have made one of these for me. I haven't heard this song in forever." Patti tapped her thumbs on the steering wheel to *You Oughta Know.* "I forgot how much I love Alanis Morrissette."

11

"She does have some great songs." I leaned my head back and was transported back to our last summer together. Before everything changed.

Chapter Four

PATTI

"Hey, wake up. I'm lonely." I pushed on Cate's shoulder.

She opened her eyes and yawned. "How long have I been sleeping?"

"For a couple states." I turned down the music and pulled into the rest stop. "Let's get something to eat. I'm starving. I ate the last granola bar a few hundred miles ago."

"How much longer?" Cate stretched and rolled her shoulders.

"If we grab something for the road, we should be there in about two hours." I picked up my purse and got out of the car. "I've got to pee, too. It's a bitch to get old."

"Watch it, I'm older than you." Cate shut her door and shuffled behind me.

"Yeah, by a week." I waddled the rest of the way to the bathroom. "There better not be a line in there. I don't know if I'm going to make it."

"I'll push them off for you." Cate held the door open as I brushed by her.

13

JESSICA AIKEN-HALL

'Oh, I see you've gotten feisty. I like it." I made my way to an open stall.

'I don't know if it's feisty or I just don't care anymore." Cate closed the door next to mine.

'Fake it 'til you make it, baby. Don't let the world get you down." I pulled out my phone and noticed a missed call from Danny. "Typical."

'What?" I heard the squeak of Cate's door. 'You alright in there?"

'Yeah, just Danny being his usual wonderful self. Husband of the year you know." The hot water on my hands warmed my bitterness. 'Don't get me wrong, I do love him. He's the father of my kids, he works hard, he's handsome."

'But?" The air dryer blew a loud puff of hot air as Cate and I waved our hands under it.

'But he can't keep it in his pants, and he drinks too much." I flicked the rest of the water off my hands before wiping them on my pants. 'See, he's the full package."

'Patti." Cate's sympathetic tone masked her disappointment.

'What?" I forced a smile to fight back the tears. 'It's fine. I'm fine."

'You deserve more than fine. You deserve better than that. If my life wasn't such a mess I'd go back to Jersey and kick his ass. Twice."

'Twice?" I held the door open as she walked past me.

'Yeah, once for keeping you away from me and the other for not treating you like the queen that you are." Cate linked arms with me.

'It's not all his fault that I haven't come home. It's just easier to stay there."

14

DEPENDING ON YOU

"I get it. Your stuck there like I'm stuck at home. Prisoners of our own choosing." Cate picked up a bag of Cool Ranch Doritos. "Remember these?"

"Yes." I took out two bottles of diet Pepsi. "And this?"

"The perfect combination." Cate picked up a sandwich.

"We can't forget the Skittles." I juggled my items in one hand while picking up a bag of the rainbow candy.

"All we need is a good Brad Pitt movie and it would be like the old days." Cate set her items on the counter. "Here, my treat."

I emptied my arms and listened to the beeps as the clerk scanned and bagged our items. "Thanks, Cate. We should do this more often. Not just when our lives are falling apart."

Cate took the bags of our makeshift lunch. "This might be the only chance I get for a while."

"I don't think that's true." I unlocked the car and opened the door for Cate.

"I don't think I can run from this anymore. I need to own up to it if I ever want a chance at life. Even if that life is behind bars." Cate bit into a chip, and the tangy smell danced its way to my nose.

"Stop talking like that. There's no way I'm letting you go to jail. I'll hire you a lawyer if I have to." I took a chip and savored the flavor as it coated my tongue.

"There's no way I'm allowing that." Cate twisted off the cap to her soda before taking a drink. "You have a family. I'm not your charity case anymore."

"What's that supposed to mean? You're not a charity case. I love you, Cate, and I don't want anything to happen to you."

"Yeah, well, maybe this is what I deserve. I killed a man. I should pay for it." Cate sighed. "It's all I can think about. And

15

JESSICA AIKEN-HALL

now that his kid is involved, I think it's time I take responsibility. I took him from his son. I had no idea he was a father."

"His kid?" My heart rate increased. "He had a kid?"

"Yeah, that's why the case was reopened." Cate rubbed her fingers to get the crumbs off. "His son is in Lawrenceville right now demanding answers. I can't make him suffer. I already stole so much from him."

"His son? How old is he? How come we've never heard about him before? It doesn't add up. Why now?" I wiped my hands off and put the car in drive.

"He didn't know about his dad, or the murder until recently. He was adopted and when he started searching for his birth parents the DNA database matched Trevor as his father." Cate handed me half of a ham salad sandwich. "He's still looking for his birth mother."

"Why would he want to open a closed case? Doesn't he know that his father was a piece of shit? You did the world a favor." Anger heated my blood. "What does the kid want? Money? I have some he can have."

"By the look of things, he doesn't need money. He was adopted into money. I'd guess that's how he was given Trevor's name in the first place."

"I don't understand what he wants from a dead man. Has he said anything about what he's hoping to gain from all of this?" The car behind me blasted its horn at me when I changed lanes. I held up my middle finger. "Jackass."

"Whoa, calm down." Cate held on to the dash. "You're going to get us killed."

"At least we'd die together." I stepped on the accelerator and sped past a group of cars. "I think I lost him."

"You even make dying sound enjoyable." Cate held the bag

16

DEPENDING ON YOU

of chips open for me. "I'd like to at least make it back home alive so I can say goodbye to my dad."

I reached my hand over and squeezed her knee. "Oh, honey. I'll get you home to your dad. I'm so sorry he's not doing well."

Cate blinked the tears out of her eyes. "I don't know what I'm going to do without him. I guess that's why I'm not worried about going to jail. Without him, what do I have?"

"You have me and Sammy and all your friends back home." I glanced over at Cate long enough to see the look of disgust on her face.

"Yeah, all my friends." She pushed out her breath. "And Sammy is on my last nerve. Were we that dumb when we were twenty-three?"

I couldn't hold in my laughter. "See, that's why I'm glad I was an only child. Except now that my parents are dead, I feel lost in the world. It's a weird feeling."

"I'll join you at the orphan club soon." Cate rolled up the bag of chips and tossed them in the backseat. "At least we have each other."

"It doesn't get any better than that." I held my hand out.

Cate took my hand and started swinging it. "What would it have been like if you didn't move away?"

"It would've been amazing. We were hot back in the day. We could have gotten a place together and vowed to never marry anyone so it would just be the two of us."

"Well, I kept up my end of the bargain." Cate snorted and covered her nose. "Oh man, I don't remember the last time I've laughed so hard." She leaned her head back. "It was when you were home for your mom's funeral."

"Yeah, that was a blast." I shook my head. "But you're right. I'm my happiest with you, even when life sucks."

17

"It's nice." Cate squeezed my hand. "You're my person."

"Ditto." For the first time in years, my cheeks hurt from smiling. "Can we make a pact that we'll make sure we get together at least twice a year from now on? We're not getting any younger. I don't want to live any more of my life miserable."

"As long as you're willing to visit me at the big house." Cate sighed. "How long do you think I'll get for murder? Do you think I'll get any credit for time served?"

"I don't think that's how it works, but you don't need to worry about it. You're not going to jail. You were at the wrong place at the wrong time. They don't have any evidence that puts you there. The case was closed twenty years ago, they're just going to humor the kid and that will be it." I turned the music back on. "What number should I play?"

"Five is my favorite." Cate hit the button until *Chumbawamba* started playing. "This song always makes me happy."

"Oh my god, is this Tubthumping?" I increased the volume. "I love this song." We sang along to the lyrics and danced to the beat.

"If we could pick a song to be our song, what would it be?" Cate turned the volume down.

"Easy. *Depending on You.*"

"Wow, that was fast." Cate flipped through the songs. "That one's not on here, *Mary Jane's Last Dance* is the only Tom Petty song on this CD."

"Oh, I love that song. Put it on." I bounced in my seat as I waited to hear Tom's voice blast through the speakers.

"I see you're still in love." Cate cranked the volume.

I hit my hand against the wheel and belted along to the song. "We should get high."

"That's a horrible idea. You're a mom and my dying father's

DEPENDING ON YOU

a cop." Cate smiled. "It could be fun. If I end up in jail, how about you smuggle me in some and then you can share the cell with me? We'd get to live together after all."

"If that means I don't have to cook, it's something I could get behind." I turned my signal to get off the highway. "Almost home."

"I don't know if I can do this." Cate turned the volume down. "What am I going to tell my dad? I..."

"About what?"

"Everything. I don't think I can lie to him anymore. Besides, when he dies, he's going to know the truth. I won't be able to hide it from him then."

"You don't tell him anything. Enjoy your time with him while you can." I put my hand on her knee. "Promise me you're not going to tell anyone anything."

"I don't know if I can keep that promise any longer." Cate's smile faded into a frown. "I've held on to this for too long."

"Give me a little time. I'm depending on you."

Chapter Five
CATE

Sammy's car wasn't in the driveway when we arrived. "You've got to be kidding me." I rolled my eyes. "I knew I couldn't depend on her. She's such a child."

"To be fair, she kind of is." Patti put the car in park and put her hand on my arm. "Take a deep breath and shake it off. We'll get him what he needs when we get inside."

"If he's still alive." The thought of walking in and finding my father dead gnawed at me.

"He is. I know it. He's a tough old guy." Patti took the keys out and handed them to me. "Let's go surprise him."

"He's going to love seeing you. I think he's missed you as much as I have." I got out of the car and shook my hands at my sides. "Ready?"

Patti took my hand. "I am."

Dad was sleeping in his hospital bed when I opened the door. I turned to Patti and put my finger to my lips. I took her bags and set them by the door. Patti stayed behind as I walked to the side of his bed. I rubbed his arm. "Dad. Dad, it's Cate. I'm home now."

20

DEPENDING ON YOU

He opened one eye and smiled. "Catie Cat."

"Hey Dad." I held the back of my hand to his forehead. "How are you feeling?"

"I'm alive. Guess that's better than the alternative." He picked up his head. "Did I die and go to heaven?"

"Hi, Mr. Silver." Patti joined me at his bedside.

"What do I owe the pleasure?" He lifted his hand to his mouth and coughed.

"It's so good to see you." Patti put her hand on his arm.

Dad's eyes connected with Patti's. "I thought I'd be seeing you." His lips turned up.

"Of course." Patti matched his smile. "It's been too long."

"Do me a favor. When I kick the bucket don't abandon Cate. She's going to need you. Now more than ever."

"Dad." I took a step back and watched their connection. Their bond was stronger than I remembered. "Don't guilt her into being my friend."

"I'm not. She needs to hear the truth. You need her and she needs you. It's not rocket science. Life's too short to walk away from what you two share." He put his hand to his chest. "You only have one chance to live, don't waste a minute of it."

"Can I get you something to eat?" I glanced around his bed. "When did Sammy leave?"

Dad shrugged. "I don't know. I told her to go. Don't be upset with her."

"She shouldn't have even asked. She knew it was her turn to stay with you," I scoffed.

"She's doing her best. I don't want to take you away from your lives. If you can live, you should. Don't sit here and watch me die."

"You're not dying, Dad. Not any time soon." I turned to

21

walk away. "What can I get you?" In the kitchen I leaned on the counter and sucked back the tears. A mixture of anger and anxiety swam around inside me. I poured him a glass of orange juice and wiped my eyes with a paper towel. The sink full of dishes was more than I could handle. I stuffed my hand in my mouth and bit down as I screamed.

"Is everything alright in here?" Patti stood in the doorway.

My lip quivered. "I can't do this. It's too much." The juice spilled onto the sticky floor as my hand shook.

Patti took the glass out of my hand and wrapped her arms around me. "I'll help get this place cleaned up. Go spend some time with your dad."

"No, you're not here to clean up my messes. Not these or any of them." I threw my hands in the air.

"I want to help. Let me. Go put on a funny movie or something and I'll order us a pizza." She handed me the juice and pushed me in the direction of the door. "Don't make me come in there."

"I don't know how to repay you."

"You already have." She blew me a kiss. "Love you, Catie Cat."

"You're something else, Patti Melt." I covered my mouth to catch the laughter.

"Get out of here before I throw something at you." Patti shooed me out of the room.

I held the cup of juice in front of Dad. "Here, at least drink this for me."

Dad nodded and complied. "This is backwards, you know."

I looked down at his T-shirt and pulled at the fabric. "I don't think so."

He swatted at my hand. "Not that, foolish. This." He

DEPENDING ON YOU

pointed at the glass in my hand. "I'm the one who's supposed to take care of you."

"You do, and you always have. I don't know where'd I'd be without you." I set the juice down and sat on the edge of his bed. "I don't go handing out World's Best Father mugs to just anyone. You've got to earn it. And boy, did you ever."

Dad reached for my hand. "You've been a pleasure. If they made World's Best Daughter mugs, I'd get you one." He laughed. "Don't tell Sammy, she'd be heartbroken."

I rolled my eyes. "I doubt she'd even notice."

"Don't be so hard on her. She's been through a lot." Dad rested his head into his pillow. "I should have done better for her. Poor kid."

"That's not true. You did everything for her. You still do. It's time she does something for herself." I looked around the room and noticed Sammy's stuff strewn all over the place.

"She's still so young. There's plenty of time for her to grow up."

"She's had plenty of time. I was way more mature when I was her age."

Dad took my hand. "Cate, you two are not the same. You've always been stronger, more reliable, dependable. But Sammy has always needed someone behind her cheering her on." His faded blue eyes looked into mine. "I need you to promise me you'll pick up where I left off."

I hung my head. "Ugh. I was afraid that was what you were going to ask me." With a sigh I turned to look at his pleading face. "Fine. I'll take care of Sammy. But only because you asked me."

"You girls should try to get along. You're the last two left."

23

"That's not true. You're still here." I leaned down and put my head on his chest. "I don't want you to leave me."

Dad put his hand on my head and caressed my hair. "I'll never really be gone. I'll always be with you."

"You promise?" I pressed my head closer and let the beat of his heart bring me comfort.

"Of course."

"Don't forget about me." Patti stood in the doorway wiping her hands on a kitchen towel. "I'm only a phone call away."

"Get over here, kid." Dad held his hand out for her to join us. "Can I count on you to take care of my Catie?"

"Absolutely. I'll even help her with Sammy." Patti perched on the side of the bed. "I'll do whatever I can to make you proud, Mr. Silver."

"Everything is going to be alright." Dad brushed his hand across my face. "You're stronger than you know. Both of you girls are."

"I hope you're right." I reached over Dad and took Patti's hand. "It's easier when we do it together."

"Don't forget that when things get tough." Patti squeezed my hand. "You're not in this life alone."

"That's my girls." Love lit up his face.

Having Patti here was the first part of making things fall into place. If only there was a way to rewind time and change how things played out. If everything happens for a reason, I haven't figured it out yet.

Summer
of
1998

Chapter Six

PATTI

I dangled my feet off the rock, letting them dip into the cool river water. "I wish the sun would stay out for more than five minutes."

"Yeah, well, it's May. Take what you can get." Cate pushed her hands deeper into the pouch on her sweatshirt.

"I demand the sun to shine down on me." I held my hands out and tilted my face to the sky.

"You're such a dork." Cate laughed. "Have you had enough yet? I'm cold."

"And you're such a baby." I steadied myself on the boulder and stood up, taking a giant leap onto the grass. "I guess we can go home if you want."

"We don't have to go home, but let's save the swimming for when it's actually warm." Cate jumped up and down. "I can't believe you put your feet into the water already. You're going to catch pneumonia."

I leaned against her as I wiped off my feet to put my socks and shoes back on. "That's not how you get pneumonia. Didn't you learn anything in Science?"

DEPENDING ON YOU

"Nope, and I probably won't the rest of the year." Cate's shoulders lifted. "Maybe if the teacher were hotter, I'd pay attention."

"Oh yeah?" I raised my brow. "How's that working for you in English?"

"I'm acing it." Cate cackled. "Looks like I'm on to something, huh?"

"Think of how good you'd do if he unbuttoned his shirt a few more buttons."

Cate wiggled her eyebrows. "We have a few more weeks left to find out."

"He's twice your age." I bent down to tie my shoe.

"So? In a couple of months that won't matter. Age is just a number." Cate shrugged. "It's not like anything is going to happen, but it doesn't hurt to fantasize about."

"You actually think about him like that?" My nose scrunched up. "I was joking."

"Why not? He's cute and stands in front of me every day and reads poetry. Some days I'm sure he's reading directly to me."

"Barf." I stuck my tongue out. "Lawrenceville's own Romeo and Juliet."

"Oh stop, it's not like you don't think about Mr. Henders like that. I've seen the way you look at him." Cate batted her eyelashes and raised her hand. "Oh, Mr. Henders, I need help finding the square root to your pants."

Laughter took my vision as my eyes filled with tears. "Good one. I'm going to have to say that to him on the last day of school."

"Why wait? We can have a double date in the teacher's lounge." Cate linked arms with me.

27

"It's sounding better and better." I rubbed my eyes and wheezed as I remembered what she said.

"Want to go see who's hanging out in town?" Cate pushed the stray strands of her hair behind her ear.

"Sure, why not. There's nothing else to do." I put my backpack on and locked arms with her again. "Maybe Jake will be there." I jabbed at her side.

"Doubtful. He's never there." Cate kicked the stone out of the path. "But maybe Andrew is."

My cheeks felt like the sun was beating down on me. "We could try for a double date with those two."

"Yeah? You want to see them every day at school if they say no? I don't think I'm ready for that kind of humiliation yet."

"But if they say yes, think of how much fun it would be. Don't you want to take a risk and find out?" I tugged at her arm.

"Nope. It's not worth it. I can't take the rejection." Cate shook her head. "If he liked me, he would have made a move by now. I'll just keep admiring the view. At least this way he won't know why I'm gawking at him."

"We've got to start living. We graduate next month. What fun stories will we have to tell our kids?"

"First of all, I wouldn't be telling my kids any of that stuff. And second, that's really offensive. We have lots of fun stories to share." Cate huffed. "Getting laid doesn't determine if we've had fun."

"That's not what I meant. We have had plenty of fun times. There're always the good times at the cemetery. What kid won't love to hear those stories?"

Cate smacked me in the side. "You're an ass."

DEPENDING ON YOU

"What? I'm being serious. I love the time up there. It's peaceful."

"Except for the time we got drunk there. That wasn't peaceful." Cate snorted. "Remember when we got lost and we couldn't find our way out?"

"Don't remind me." I covered my face. "I can't believe I let you talk me into drinking for the first time with a bunch of dead people."

"They're the best ones to party with. Quiet and they don't want to get in your pants." Cate snickered. "Or maybe they do."

I tapped her arm. "Nothing happened. You were trying to scare me. I know it was you."

"It wasn't me. Something or someone grabbed your ass." She held her hands up. "I swear it wasn't me."

"How is that even possible?" I put my hands on my head and pulled at my hair. "I don't want to think about who it could have been." I shook my body to get rid of the chill.

"Well, if it doesn't work out with Jake and Andrew we know where to go." Cate put her hands on her thighs and laughed. "Cheap prom date." She put her arm out. "Look, take our picture." She plastered on a huge smile.

"I'm not so sure I want to go back there anymore." I shook my head.

"Oh, you know I'm only teasing. That's our place. It's not creepy. Besides, if you were a ghost would you want to hang out with your dead body?" She shook her head. "No, you'd want to follow the people you loved or the ones who did you wrong."

"True. I'd follow Andrew around and make sure he never had sex with anyone else." I crossed my arms.

29

"You do know you have to be dead first, right?" Cate raised her brow.

"I don't want to be dead, it's only if I were." I linked my arm through hers. "Come on, let's go see if there are any boys on this side of the ground we can try our luck with."

"Let's make a pact."

"Alright." I turned to look at her. "What kind?"

"Let's make it our mission to lose our virginity this summer." Cate held her hand at her side. "That way we can make the memory together, and not while you're off at college."

I nodded as I thought about her plan. "I like the sound of that."

"We can make our first goal to have a date we wouldn't mind doing for prom."

I pointed to the sky. "First mission, find hot, horny boys."

"They don't even have to be hot." Cate shrugged. "Think of how that opens up the playing field."

"Nope." I waved my finger. "I'm not giving it up to some homely guy. He's got to be somewhat attractive or it's not going to work for me."

"Whatever floats your boat." Cate twisted her face. "When August rolls around you might feel differently."

"I won't. I don't want to picture some ugly dude every time someone asks me about my first time."

"How often do you think that's going to come up in conversation?" Cate deepened her voice. "Excuse me, can you give me a play by play of the first time you did the nasty?"

"I don't know. All I know is I want it to be somewhat special and spreading my legs to the first willing guy doesn't sound special. We could make it happen right now."

"How?" Cate asked.

DEPENDING ON YOU

"Hold up a sign. Desperate girls looking for love."

"It might come to that." Cate grinned. "I'm only kidding. You're beautiful. Any guy would be lucky to have you, any part of you."

"Same goes for you." I pushed the hair behind my ear. "We'll keep our standards set high and make it happen. Summer of sex is about to begin."

Chapter Seven

CATE

The sound of broken glass pulled me out of bed. I pressed my ear to my door to see what was going on. My heart shot up into my throat when I heard the footsteps get closer. I rushed back to my bed and pulled the sheet over my head. The hallway light crept into my room as the door opened.

"What are you doing, you lazy, good for nothing whore?" My light flickered on and off. "I said, what are you doing?"

I squeezed my eyes tight and tried not to react. I didn't want her to know I was awake. I held my breath, waiting for her to get bored and leave.

The clicking of my light switch being turned on and off almost pulled me out of possum. "Must be nice to sleep all day." I remained still even after my door slammed. There was still a chance she was in my room.

I perked my ears up to listen for every sound I could detect. Silence danced around me. It was too quiet. I knew that meant she was up to something else. I opened one eye and scanned the room. She wasn't in there. I placed my hand on my chest to try

32

DEPENDING ON YOU

to calm the palpitations lifting my shirt. Mom was so unpredictable, and predictable at the same time.

I never know what is going to set her off, but once she's provoked, she follows the same routine. First, she picks someone to target. Lately it's been Dad and me. Thankfully it hasn't been Sammy. Once she sets her sight on the enemy, she sets out to destroy them. Throwing or breaking stuff you love and then the yelling and name calling. Some days I'm a bitch, other days I'm a whore.

Over the years, I've learned not to engage when she's in one of her moods. It makes her mad at first, but after a while she gives up. As I've gotten older, she seems to hate me more. When I was younger there would be days she showed me she loved me, but she hasn't hugged or said anything nice since before Sammy was born.

I rolled out of bed and turned off the light she left on and locked my door. She'll be pissed if she tries to come back in, but it was a risk I was willing to take. At my window the full moon poured its light down over me. I closed my eyes and soaked up the beauty. If only life was as pure as this.

I tossed and turned in bed when I thought about how much I missed the mom I used to have. The only good thing was she was good to Sammy. She hadn't been mean to her yet, and I needed to keep it that way.

Headlights pulled into the driveway, but Dad wasn't due to be home for at least another three hours. I crawled back out of bed and pulled my curtain back. Mom was leaning into the side of the pickup. I couldn't see what she was doing, but it looked like she was kissing someone. The noise from the truck was too loud, making it impossible to hear what they were saying.

I continued watching, waiting to see something worth

33

worrying about. Mom hasn't cheated on Dad since Sammy was born, at least not openly. This behavior wasn't new. My entire childhood was filled with holding secrets for my mom and meeting lots of uncles. I was dumb enough to believe my mother. Never again. When the dots started clicking, I stopped swallowing the lies she fed me. I'd rather starve.

Mom had something in her hand when she left her visitor. I squinted trying to see what it was. She stuffed the small package into her back pocket and turned to blow a kiss to the person driving away. I tiptoed back to bed and laid back down. My imagination led me down all kinds of rabbit holes as to what Mom shoved into her pocket. I looked over at my phone on my desk trying to will enough strength to call Dad and tell him what took place in our driveway or how Mom was at it again. But I couldn't. I didn't want to be the reason he finally had enough and walked away. I couldn't deal with Mom and Sammy on my own. At least Dad took some of the blows for me.

The war between doing what was right and keeping the peace was at it again, pulling apart my insides. I'd vowed to never hold anymore secrets, but if I didn't know what I saw, there was nothing to tell. At least that was what I kept telling myself. If Mom starts using again, I might as well kiss my life goodbye. Living with her like that is not worth the heartache. I'd either have to kidnap Sammy or try to convince Dad to leave. Neither scenario was an option.

I did my best to hear what she was up to, but the night was still. Her yelling and thrashing ended. Silence with Mom was not a good thing. It meant the arrow on her crazy scale tipped sides and she was either on a dive into depression or shooting up. I could only hope for the dark days to return. There's no

DEPENDING ON YOU

way I had another one of her drug-induced sprees in me. Pieces of me were still recovering from her last.

Cries from Sammy jerked me out of the spiral I was falling into. Without thought, I jumped to my feet and made my way to her room. Her blanket was balled up around her and her pajamas I had put her in before bed were half off. "Sammy? What's wrong?"

She whimpered and held her arms up. "Sissy."

I scooped her up in my arms and brought her back to my room, making sure she had her magic blanket with her. The one I gave her to hug when I'm at Patti's. "You want to sleep with me?" I lowered her onto my bed.

She nodded with her thumb jammed into her mouth. I held the blankets open for her to crawl under and joined her. She wrapped her spindly arms around my neck and pushed herself as close to me as she could get. "Don't go."

"I'm not going anywhere." I pushed her hair off her sweaty forehead. "Go to sleep."

"I'm not tired. I don't want to sleep." The sound of her pounding heart was louder than her voice.

"It's late, Sammy. If you go to sleep maybe we can go see Patti at the ice cream shop tomorrow."

"Okay." She nuzzled her head into my chest. Her breathing slowed as she settled into me. "I love ice cream. And Patti."

"Me, too." I kissed the top of her head and drifted off to sleep with her in my arms. I'd do whatever it took to shield her from the mother I grew up with. She deserved the kind of mom on TV that offered love and laughter.

35

Chapter Eight

PATTI

Mom poured the milk over my cereal before sitting across the table from me. "I'm going to miss this." She rested her chin in her hand as she gazed at me.

"What? Me eating Cheerios?" I guided the spoon full of sweet circles into my mouth.

She laughed. "Well yes, but also just having you around. What am I going to do with myself when you're gone? Who am I going to cook for? Watch movies with?"

"Mom, I'm not dying. I'll be home on the weekends and on all of my breaks." I pushed around the contents of my bowl. "It won't be that bad."

"I know. I want you to have fun and experience new things." She pushed up her cheeks. "Don't worry about me. I'll be fine."

"Mom." I looked up at her. "Please don't make me feel guilty. It's already hard enough to leave you and Cate behind."

"Honey, don't feel guilty. It's important that you spread

DEPENDING ON YOU

your wings and fly out of the nest. I'll be fine." She put her hand on my arm and gave it a squeeze. "And so will Cate."

"Maybe I should look into going to the community college. That way I can stay here with you. I'd still be getting an education." I lifted my shoulders. "I can call them and see if there's still time."

"No. You've had your heart set on going away to college since you were a little girl. Don't give up on your dreams for anyone."

"What if I hate it there? What if I don't make any friends? What if I can't handle college?" I dropped my spoon. "I don't think I'm ready."

"Patti, you'll do great things. It's normal to be afraid and even homesick. I'm only a phone call and an eight-hour drive away. It's going to be fun." She got up and poured me a glass of orange juice. "Drink up, you're going to be late for work."

I glanced over at the microwave clock and emptied the glass in one big gulp. "Thanks Mom, for everything."

"That's what moms are for." She wiped her hands off on her apron. "Have a good day at work, honey. Do you and Cate have plans tonight?"

"I'm not sure what we have planned." I blew her a kiss and went out the door. College sounded more fun when it was years away, but now that it was just around the corner, I'm not sure I made the right decision. I know Mom wishes I'd stay home but she doesn't want to be the reason I don't go.

I kicked at a pebble on the sidewalk and blew out my apprehension. If Dad were still alive, it would be easier to leave Mom behind. I didn't even consider him dying a possibility. I wiped the side of my eyes with my sleeve and tried to push the thoughts about Dad out of my mind. I took the Walkman out

37

of my backpack and put the headphones on my head. As I waited for the CD to load, I zipped my bag closed and put it on my back.

The sun was shining bright today. Summer was on the way. I closed my eyes and held my face up to the sun, letting its rays wash away my pain. The grief comes in waves, pounding down over me like the water crashing into the rocks. Nowhere around one minute and the next it's more than I can take.

Jewel's voice soothed my soul as I continued to the ice cream stand. Cate and Sammy were sitting on the bench under the oak tree. I turned off the music and walked over to them. "What are you guys doing here so early?" I fished the key out of my backpack.

"I promised Sammy some ice cream and a visit with her favorite person." Cate bounced Sammy on her knee.

"Patti!" Sammy shrieked and held out her arms.

I traded Cate my key for her little sister. "Sammy!" I kissed her cold cheek. "You should sit in the sun. It's going to be a beautiful day." I spun her around letting her hair fly behind her.

"Again!" Sammy held her legs tight against my hips.

"If I'm dizzy, who's going to get you ice cream?" I scrunched up my nose.

"She can." Sammy pointed at Cate.

"I don't think so." Cate put her hands on her hips. "We don't want to get Patti fired."

I reached for the key. "Do you want to help me?"

Sammy shook her head with her mouth in an open smile. "Ice cream."

"You're silly." I moved her to my hip as I unlocked the door. "What will it be Miss Sammy?"

"Chocolate." Sammy kicked her feet at my sides.

DEPENDING ON YOU

"A girl after my own heart." I put Sammy on the ground and took her hand. "Come on, let's get you some ice cream.

Cate followed behind us. "I don't think this is a good idea. What if someone see us in here?"

"Who in their right mind is going to be getting ice cream at nine in the morning? It's not exactly ice cream weather." I shrugged. "It's not like I care if I get fired."

"You need this job so you can have money for college." Cate crossed her arms as she scanned our surroundings.

"Hey, don't worry about it. We'll be quick." I opened the cooler and took out the tub of chocolate ice cream. "How about I scoop and you can put the toppings on?"

Sammy jumped up and down eyeing my every move. I handed her a bowl before filling one for Cate. "Looks like Sissy needs some, too."

"Thanks." Cate sighed. "Ice cream fixes everything."

"Most." I handed her the bowl. "What's up? Why do you look so sad?"

Cate widened her eyes and nodded toward Sammy. "Oh nothing. The same reason as always."

I put another scoop in their bowls. "Here, let's make these doubles."

"It's getting bad again, Patti. I thought these days were behind us. It's not..." Cate looked down at Sammy who had topping spilling out of her dish. "I just wanted better for Sammy."

"What can I do to help?" I leaned on the counter and watched Sammy stuff her spoon into her mouth.

"Nothing. It's not your job." Cate squeezed her eyes closed. "I need to figure out what to do."

"Cate, you're not alone. You have me."

39

"Yeah, well, you have enough on your mind. You don't need my drama." Cate stabbed her spoon into her ice cream.

"It's not drama. You don't deserve to be stressed out over this stuff. Have you talked to your dad?"

"Not yet. I wanted to get out of the house before she woke up and Dad was sleeping. He picked up a late shift last night." Cate took a big bite, spilling some onto her shirt.

"But you're going to, right?" I folded my arms. "You're not going to carry this by yourself. Because if you don't talk to him, I will."

"No, don't do that. I'll tell him. I'm done keeping secrets for her. I just want to find the right time. Besides, you don't even know what's going on."

"I have a good idea. And I bet your dad does, too. He's not dumb. He's lived with her long enough to know..."

"He's been working a lot of extra shifts. He's hardly ever home and when he is, he's sleeping." Cate set her dish on the counter. "I'll talk to him, I promise."

I wiped the chocolate off the counter with a wet rag. "You better." I looked down at Sammy. "You're lucky to have Cate as your big sister."

"She's lucky, too." Sammy grinned as she danced around her melting dish of ice cream.

"You're right. I am." Cate took a napkin and cleaned off Sammy's face. "Why don't we finish this outside?"

"I'm full." Sammy rubbed her belly.

"You ate almost the whole bowl, no wonder your tummy hurts." I took her bowl and tossed it in the trash.

Cate handed me her dish. "I'm full, too."

"I expected more from you." I waved my finger at her. "Who are you? Letting chocolate go to waste."

DEPENDING ON YOU

"I tried, but you gave me the whole box." Cate picked Sammy up. "Do you want to go see if Daddy's awake?"

Sammy shook her head and clung to Cate.

"It will be okay, Sammy. You and Cate have each other." I rubbed Sammy's back. "If you want, maybe you guys can come over to my house tonight. We can order pizza and watch movies."

Cate pushed Sammy's hair out of her face. "That sounds fun, doesn't it?"

Sammy's face lit up. "At Patti's house?"

"Yeah, we can have a girl's night. Just the three of us. Well, and my mom, but she's fun." I opened the door and gave Cate a pat on the back as she walked past me. "I love you girls. See you later."

Chapter Nine
CATE

I set Sammy in the chair and turned the TV on for her. "You stay here and I'll be right back." I pointed the remote to turn up the volume before leaving the living room.

Sammy curled up in her usual spot and sang along with the cartoon characters. With slow, small steps I walked around the table to make sure not to wake Mom up, who was snoring with her head on the kitchen table. Dad's cruiser was in the driveway, so I knew he was still in the house someplace.

I stood in front of the bedroom door and put my hand up to knock before lowering it. The last thing I wanted to do was wake him up after working a double shift. But with Mom asleep, it was the perfect time. I turned the doorknob, opening the door just enough to slip through. The blanket was pulled up to Dad's nose. My heart raced as I gathered my thoughts.

I wiggled his foot. "Dad." He didn't stir. I walked over to the head of the bed and bent down to get right above his head. "Dad."

He sprang up, hitting my nose. "Is everything alright?"

DEPENDING ON YOU

I held my finger to my lips. "I need to talk to you."

Dad sat up and blinked his eyes. "What's going on?"

"It's Mom," I whispered looking behind me to make sure she wasn't there. "She's getting out of control again."

"What's she doing?"

I pulled my eyes away from his. "I think she's using again."

"Why do you think that?" He pushed the blankets off and sat on the edge of the bed with me.

"She's been acting... scary lately. She's yelling and smashing stuff." I pulled my hand into my sleeve.

"Well, you know your mom acts like that. It doesn't mean she's doing anything wrong." Dad scratched his head.

"And I saw her in the driveway talking to someone late last night."

"Someone was here? Last night?" He shook his head. "What kind of car was it?"

"I don't know. It was a truck, but that's all I know. It was dark and I didn't want her to know I was watching her."

"Did he come inside?" Dad rubbed his hand over his face.

"No, he stayed outside. She was with him for a while, but she didn't get in the truck with him. When she was coming back inside, I saw her put something in her back pocket." I wrung my hands. "I didn't dare come out of my room to see what she had."

Dad put his hand on my knee. "That's not your job. I'm glad you stayed in your room." He tossed his head back. "I'll see what I can find out."

"I'm sorry. I didn't know how to tell you, but I don't want things to turn into the last time. I don't want Sammy to grow up like this." I hung my head.

"Oh, Catie Cat. You can tell me anything. There are no

43

secrets between us. No matter what. Do you understand?" He pushed the hair behind my ear.

I nodded. "I didn't want to bother you. I wanted to take care of it on my own, but it's happening so fast this time."

"This isn't something you need to do on your own. I'm glad you told me. Thank you for trusting me."

"Is it alright if Sammy and I spend the night at Patti's tonight?"

"You want Sammy to go with you?" Dad raised his brow.

"It was Patti's idea. She asked Sammy already. If I don't take her with me, she's going to be heartbroken."

"As long as you want to deal with your baby sister all night, it's fine with me. It will give me time to have a talk with your mother." Dad rubbed my back. "I love you, Catie Cat. You're a good big sister."

"I'm scared, Dad." I leaned into his side. "I don't want it to go back to the way it used to. She's getting out of control again. I don't want Sammy to be afraid of Mom. It's not fair."

Dad wrapped his arm around me. "I know. I'll take care of it."

I wanted to believe him, but I've heard it all before. He likes to see the good in people. Even with all his years of being a detective, he still believes there is good in everyone. He doesn't think anyone can be all bad. With Mom, I think he's wrong. I want him to be right, but I know better.

MRS. THOMAS OPENED the door as soon as she saw Sammy and I on the front porch. "Hi, girls, I'm so excited to see you both." She patted Sammy on the head.

DEPENDING ON YOU

"Thanks for letting us come over." I set our bags on the floor.

"You know you're always welcome here. Sammy is, too. I'm going to be lonely when Patti leaves for college, so we'll have to plan some more fun nights together." She took Sammy's hand. "Do you want to go see all the fun snacks we have for tonight?"

Sammy squealed. "Yeah."

Mrs. Thomas swung Sammy's hand as they walked into the kitchen.

"Hey." Patti picked up one of our bags. "I think my mom's more excited than all of us combined."

"I don't know, Sammy looks pretty happy, too."

"I think Mom wishes they had another baby. She's having a hard time with me leaving. I sort of want to wait a year or two before I leave, but she won't let me." Patti tossed the bag on her bed.

"Yeah, she told me we're welcome here anytime. It'd be weird to hang out here without you." I stepped over the pillows on the floor. "What's this?"

"Oh, that?" Patti laughed. "Mom told me to make a fort for us to sleep in. I thought it'd be fun if we made it together."

"That does sound like fun." I picked up a pillow. "Remember when I used to make forts in your backyard?"

Patti nodded. "I do. My dad loved when we were out there having fun. I think he built more of them than we ever did."

"I miss him." I tossed the pillow back onto the pile. "I'm sorry, I shouldn't..."

"No, don't be sorry. I miss him, too. He loved you just as much as he loved me. We were his girls." Patti sat on her bed. "I'm worried about Mom being all alone."

45

"Don't worry. I'll keep her company." I sat next to Patti. "My mom is using again."

"Oh, Cate." Patti put her hand on my back. "How do you know?"

"There was some guy in our driveway last night. She was kissing him and when she walked away, she had something in her hand. I don't know what it was, but I saw her hide it in her pocket."

"Did you tell your dad?" Patti picked at the blanket. "Can't he do something about it?"

"I told him, but I'm not sure what good it will do. You know how he is. He wants to save the world, no matter the cost."

"That's not a bad thing, Cate. Your dad is a good guy. I know he wants what's best for you all, even your mom."

"Yeah, I know he loves her, but I need his help. I don't know if I can deal with another incident." I sat on my hands. "I can't always wonder who's going to be at the house, or if she's going to ignore me or try to kill me."

"If it gets bad, bring Sammy here. You can use my room whenever you need to. Even if you just want someplace to hide. Mom won't bother you. She'd just be happy to have you here."

"Thanks." I fell back onto the bed. "I don't want to think about you leaving right now. I wish I could go with you."

"I know, me, too. But I understand why you can't. Sammy needs you. Can you imagine what her life would be like without you?" Patti turned to look at me. "I'm sorry, that was stupid."

"No, it's fine. I know what you meant. And that's why I can't leave her, because I know what would happen if I did." I sighed. "I guess we'll just have to make these next few weeks count."

DEPENDING ON YOU

Patti joined me on the bed, pressing her forehead against mine. "You know what I forgot to tell you?"

"What?"

"Jake started at the ice cream shop today."

I took her hand and squeezed. "Oh my god, really?"

"Yup. I get to train him. Looks like you and Sammy are going to have to come get even more ice cream."

"Maybe you can put in a good word for me," I said with a smile on my face that lit up my eyes.

"Already started." She sat up and pushed the hair out of her eyes. "Well, sort of. I wanted to be subtle. Feel things out first."

I kicked her feet and covered my face. "What did he say when you mentioned me?"

"I think he likes you." Patti shrugged. "He will by the time I'm done with him."

"Is he still friends with Andrew?" I sprung up. "This could be perfect. Just what we needed to happen."

She nodded. "I know. I'm looking forward to Andrew coming to visit Jake soon."

"All the ice cream is going to melt with Jake around. He's so hot." I batted my eyes. "So are you, of course."

"You'll have to come lick it up." Patti tossed a pillow at me. "I know what your new favorite flavor is."

"I can't wait for summer to start now." I frowned. "Well, I can. I don't want school to end because it will be our last time in the same school for the rest of our lives."

"Hey." She took my hands. "We will make the best of it. And like you said, let's make this the best summer ever."

"Deal." I lowered my shoulders. "You know we waited our whole life for senior year, and now it's going so fast. Graduation is less than a month away."

47

JESSICA AIKEN-HALL

"It is crazy how that works. But think of it this way, if this year has gone by so fast, imagine how fast the next four years will go."

"True. Like warp speed I hope." I snapped my fingers. "And you're back."

"Something like that." Patti laughed. "You can come visit me and I'll come home, too. We'll be together forever. Nothing will come between us."

Chapter Ten

CATE

Sammy and Mrs. Thomas were already up watching cartoons and eating pancakes in the living room when Patti and I got up. "How long have you been up?" I stood in the doorway of the living room and rubbed the sleep from my eyes.

Sammy lifted her shoulders as she shoveled the fork into her mouth.

"We've been up for a while. But to be fair, I did wake her up." Mrs. Thomas leaned forward and wiped the syrup off Sammy's chin.

I tilted my head, unable to keep the smile off my face. "Thanks for being so good to her."

Mrs. Thomas pushed closer to Sammy on the couch, bumping her knee on the TV tray. "No, thank you girls for spending the night with me. It was a lot of fun hearing the laughter. And it was even better to have someone to watch cartoons with." She wrapped her arm around Sammy.

"Mom, did you make any pancakes for us?" Patti slammed the refrigerator door closed.

49

JESSICA AIKEN-HALL

"They're in the oven, staying warm. No one wants cold pancakes." Mrs. Thomas didn't pull her attention away from the TV. "Look, Sammy, those bears are having breakfast, too."

Sammy giggled. "They like pancakes, too."

"Thanks, Mom." Patti calmed down when she pulled the plate out of the oven.

"I haven't had a hot breakfast in ages." I pulled out a chair and sat down. "This is nice. Look how happy they are in there."

"I know." Patti rolled her eyes. "Looks like I've been replaced."

"Sammy has a way of stealing the show, but you haven't been replaced. Your mom would never do that." I poured the syrup over the stack on my plate.

"I know. I was kidding. I haven't seen Mom this happy since Dad died." Patti handed me a glass of orange juice. "See why you guys need to come over here when I'm gone?"

I nodded. "We will, especially if she keeps making us these things."

Mrs. Thomas appeared in the kitchen with two empty plates. "What are you girls up to today?"

"I don't know yet. I have the day off." Patti took a big bite. "What do you want to do?" she asked with her mouth full.

"Maybe we could go to the movies?" I lifted my shoulders. "I don't know how Sammy will act in the theater, though."

"I'll keep her with me." Mrs. Thomas wiped her hands off on the towel hanging off the stove. "I was thinking I should start planning a birthday party and I'd love the help."

"She's not all that helpful in stores." I looked in the living room and saw Sammy curled up in the blanket, but this time it wasn't like she was hiding from anything. This time she was completely at ease.

50

"Oh, I'm sure she's fine." Mrs. Thomas smiled. "I've had my fair share of shopping with unhelpful children before."

"Hey, what's that supposed to mean?" Patti looked up with her best pouty face.

"I'm only kidding, honey. I'd be happy to have Sammy join me if you girls want to go do something fun together." Mrs. Thomas reached into her purse. "Here's some money. Go enjoy the afternoon together and we can meet for dinner at Lawrenceville Pizza."

"Are you sure? I don't want to pawn her off on you all day." I looked at Patti for support, but she was too invested in her breakfast to notice.

"Sammy's my good friend. It'd be nice to have some help picking out the perfect decorations. I'd be happy to spend the day with her." Mrs. Thomas walked back to the living room. "Sammy, do you want to go shopping with me?"

Sammy turned and nodded so hard, I thought her tiny little head was going to shoot off.

"There, it's settled. We can meet for pizza after the movie. Have fun and don't worry about us." Mrs. Thomas finished cleaning up the breakfast mess while Sammy finished her show.

"Do you want to see if Jake and Andrew want to meet us at the movies?" Patti wiggled her eyebrows.

"I don't think so. Not yet. Why don't we go alone this time? We can work on a plan for a double date later, after you have more time to talk to Jake about me." I pushed myself away from the table. "I don't want to get too eager and ruin any chance I may have. He's the only one I want to complete the mission with."

"Complete the mission?" Patti spit out her juice. "That's a new one."

51

JESSICA AIKEN-HALL

"You know what I mean." I nodded in the direction of her mom. "Let's take that part slow, at least for now."

"Okay." She put her plate in the sink. "So, what do you want to go see?"

"I don't know." I shrugged. "We could watch *The Wedding Singer* again."

"Again?" Patti smirked. "Why not. At least we won't have to pay attention."

"Oh, I'll be paying attention." I wiggled my eyebrows.

"That's right, only when Adam Sandler is on the big screen." Patti flicked water at me. "Cate and Adam up in a tree."

"Knock it off. Drew Barrymore really brings out the best in him. He's hard to resist with her by his side."

"Yeah, yeah, I'm sure that's what it is." Patti raced down the hall to her room. "Come on, let's get ready."

I rushed after her. "I think we should go see my dad before we go to the movies. I want to know how last night went."

Patti handed me the phone. "Why don't you call him? That way we can get a ride with Mom."

I blew out the apprehension. "That makes more sense, doesn't it?" I sat on her bed with the cordless phone in my hand. "I'm kind of nervous. What if they didn't talk, or she lied to him?"

"You won't know until you ask." Patti joined me on the bed. "Here, let me dial it." She took the phone and pressed the numbers. "Hello, is Detective Silver in?" She jammed the phone to my ear.

"Hi, Dad?" I cleared my throat. "Is it okay if Mrs. Thomas takes Sammy shopping while Patti and I go to the movies?"

Patti jabbed me in the ribs with her elbow and mouthed "Ask him."

52

DEPENDING ON YOU

"As long as she's okay with that, I think it would be a nice idea." Dad's voice sounded tired.

I pushed her hand away and closed my eyes. "Yeah, she's okay with it, excited actually."

Patti took the phone out of my hand. "Hi, Mr. Silver, it's Patti. Cate wanted to know how the talk went last night with Mrs. Silver."

I pulled the phone out of her hand. "Dad, it's me. Sorry..."

"Don't be sorry." Dad paused. "I think we should talk in person. How about tomorrow? Do you think you girls can stay there another night?"

I looked over at Patti as I felt the tears roll down my cheeks. "I can ask."

Patti put her arm around my waist. "Tell him you can stay here as long as you want. Both of you can."

"Okay, we can stay." I dried my eyes. "Is everything okay? Are you sure I shouldn't come home now?"

"No, don't do that." The harshness of Dad's voice stung. "We can talk tomorrow. I have the morning off."

"Okay." The phone went dead before I had the chance to ask more questions, although I probably couldn't have gotten the words I wanted to say out.

Patti leaned her head on my shoulder. "I'm sorry Cate, I shouldn't have stuck my nose in it."

The weight of my head made it drop between my shoulders. "It's okay. I wanted to know."

"Try to push it out of your head for the day and let's go have some fun. Adam Sandler awaits you." She stood up and took my hands. "Go take a shower. I'll take mine after you." She handed me my backpack.

With my stuff in my hand I locked myself in the bathroom

53

and turned on the shower. As my clothes fell to the floor, I couldn't hold the emotions in. Uncertainty mixed with fear crept up my body. What did he need to tell me and why did I have to wait? Every possible scenario cascaded over me falling with the hot water. Only the water was able to be washed away, the unknown and dread lingered no matter how hard I scrubbed.

The wish I had made on the shooting star when I was seven floated back into view. I wished for a good mommy. One who would love and cherish me, but mostly wrap me in safety. Seeing Sammy with Mrs. Thomas I knew my wish had been granted. Only it was not what I had been looking for. Patti and I met right after I made that wish. Mrs. Thomas had loved me since. She was the mommy I had been searching for, even though she had been here all along.

Chapter Eleven

CATE

I was thankful for the three-day weekend. I was able to leave Sammy with Mrs. Thomas and have the talk with Dad on my own. Patti had a long day ahead of her at the ice cream shop. One of the busiest days of the year, at least that's what she said.

Relief washed over me when I saw Mom's car wasn't in the driveway, only Dad's. The kitchen was dark when I walked inside, and so was the living room. "Dad?" My voice bounced back at me off the empty walls. All of the pictures that had been hanging there were gone. "Dad?" The crunch of broken glass under my feet made my skin crawl. The last time this happened it was Dad who stepped on the glass, without his boots on. I think it was what Mom had planned. Chills shot through me as I imagined the pain I saw bring him to his knees.

Panic raced through my body as I took small, calculated steps down the hall. "Dad?" I stood by their bedroom door, with my hand on the doorknob. The creak of worn metal rubbing against the wood exaggerated the agony I was so desper-

55

JESSICA AIKEN-HALL

ately trying to erase. "Dad." My voice trembled as I squinted to see something, anything in the darkness of the room. The curtains were closed, blocking out all the outside light.

I vaulted toward the ceiling when I felt the warmth of someone's hand on my shoulder. My heart beat against my chest, causing my surroundings to disappear. I squeezed my eyes shut, hoping that what I couldn't see wouldn't hurt me.

"Catie Cat, it's me." Dad's familiar voice pulled me out of the panic I was falling into. "I'm sorry to scare you."

I turned around and fell into his arms. "I'm so glad you're here."

"Where else would I be?" He tightened his arms around me. "I was outside having my coffee. It's beautiful out there today." He took my hand and led me down the hall.

"What happened in here?"

"Oh, nothing for you to worry about. Come with me, let's go enjoy the sunshine while we talk." He slid the patio door open and stood on the deck with his neck stretched toward the sky. "I love this time of year."

"What's going on? Where's Mom?" I folded my arms and scanned the backyard. Nothing looked out of the ordinary.

Dad sighed and put his hands in his pockets. "Why don't we go sit down and talk?"

"Please just tell me." I stood, planted in place, not able to move.

"Your mother and I are taking a break for a while." He rubbed his hand over his face and let out the breath he was holding.

"A break? What does that mean?" I asked inching closer to where he was standing.

"Well, Cate, I'm not really sure." He sat down in the lawn

56

DEPENDING ON YOU

chair and leaned forward. "As you saw inside, things got a little messy. I said some things I'm not proud of. She said some things and we came to the agreement that we would spend some time apart while we figure things out."

"Where are you going?" I chewed on my fingernail as I tried to wrap my head around the idea of a life without Dad.

"I'm not going anywhere." Dad forced a smile. "Your mother took off last night."

"Took off? Where?"

"I'm not sure. She packed a couple of bags and muttered some insults before she drove away." Dad leaned back in his chair and closed his eyes. "I don't want you to think that any of this is your fault."

"What about Sammy? What are we going to tell her?" I sat on the edge of the chair next to him and thought about all the pieces I would need to pick up. "She's going to be devastated."

"I don't think she will be, not as long as she has you." Dad's shoulders fell. "I'm so sorry kiddo. I didn't want it to be this way. I tried to have a civil conversation with her, but she blew up at me."

"Dad, it's not your fault. I know how she is. I live here, too. Sammy's still going to be sad. She's not going to understand where Mom is." Frustration pushed the headache to the surface. "God, I hate her."

"You know that's not true. You're just angry right now." Dad reached for his coffee. "She just needs to get some help and she'll be good as new."

"She can't get any worse." I rolled my eyes. "We'll be better off without her. God only knows what kind of people she would have had coming over if she stayed."

57

"What does that mean?" Dad raised his brow. "I thought you said no one came inside."

"Not this time." I looked away as soon as the words slipped out.

"Not this time? What are you talking about?"

"It's nothing. I didn't mean..."

"Cate, were there people in the house that made you feel unsafe?" Dad leaned forward and touched my arm. "Look at me."

"It's nothing." I sniffled to block the memories from taking me back to that night.

"Cate. I need you to tell me what happened." The sternness of his voice made me regret saying anything. I'd managed to keep this secret for almost a decade, and in an instant, it spilled out like sour milk.

I twisted my foot in the grass. "You knew Mom had visitors."

"Yes, but I never knew anyone hurt you or Sammy. Did they? Did someone hurt one of you?" Dad inched closer to me. "Honey, please tell me what happened."

"It was a long time ago. I don't really remember." I kept my back to him. I didn't want him to look into my eyes. My words could keep the truth from him, but I knew he'd be able to see what I wasn't saying.

"Remember, you can tell me anything. No matter what. I want you to be able to come to me anytime. It's my job to protect you girls, but I can't do my job when I don't know what's going on."

"It was before Sammy was born." I sat on my hands trying to feel the pain someplace other than my heart. "I'm fine, though. You don't need to worry."

"That's why you were so afraid inside, wasn't it? That's why you're so jumpy all the time. I thought it was weird, but your mother told me I was imagining things." Dad's voice cracked. "I'm so sorry. I can't believe I let someone hurt you."

"Dad." When I turned to look at him, I saw the moisture building in his eyes. "It's not your fault."

"It is." He covered his mouth. "I had a feeling something had happened, but I didn't do anything. I trusted your mother. I shouldn't have. It's my job to protect you."

"How were you supposed to know if I never told you? I didn't tell anyone. Only Patti." I pulled my eyes away and blinked. "I was seven. Mom told me not to tell you or you'd bring me to jail. I believed her. It's my fault for thinking you would have been mad at me."

"Oh my God, you were just a baby." Dad covered his face and leaned onto his knees.

"But I'm not anymore. I'm okay now. That's because I have you." I put my hand on his back. "I love you Dad."

"You shouldn't." His body heaved under my hand. "I'm a fraud."

"No, you're not. I shouldn't have said anything. Dad, I'm okay, and Sammy will be, too, because we have you."

"I go to work every day to serve and protect and I couldn't even protect my little girl. My head was buried in the sand. I only wanted what was best for you and look what happened." He threw his hands up.

"It's fine, it wasn't that bad."

"Who was it?" Dad cracked his knuckles.

"I don't know his name. It was one of Mom's friends." I bit my bottom lip as images from that night filled my head.

"What did he look like? How often was he at the house?"

59

"I only saw him once. I don't remember what he looks like. I've tried hard to erase that night from my memory."

"What did he do to you?" Dad wrung his hands. "How did he hurt you?"

I shook my head. "I don't remember."

"Come on, Cate, please tell me what happened to you. I couldn't help you then, let me help you now."

"It's really not that big of a deal. I was seven. I didn't know what he was doing to me." I shrugged. "I'm fine, Dad. It only happened once."

"But what did he do?" Dad rocked in his chair. "Where was your mother?"

"She was watching. She told him he could get his payment from me, but I didn't know what that meant. I wasn't scared, not at first. Mom made me think I was doing her a favor. She told me it was our secret, but then after he left, she spanked me. She said if I told anyone I'd be in trouble." I stared into the trees behind our house, trying to push her voice out of my head. "She told me you would have been mad at me. I didn't want you to leave me, so I didn't tell anyone." I picked at my jeans. "When I met Patti, I told her about what happened. We were just kids, but she told me she'd never let anyone hurt me again. And she hasn't."

"I knew there was a reason I loved that girl." Dad smiled. "I'm so sorry, Cate. I wish I had known when it happened. I would have taken care of it. I guess your mom leaving was the best thing that could have happened to all of us."

"Yeah, I think so. At least now Sammy will be safe. I've been so worried about something like that happening to her, I didn't dare leave when Mom was having one of her episodes."

DEPENDING ON YOU

Dad took my hand. "You're a brave girl, Catie Cat. I'll spend the rest of my life making it up to you."

"You don't have to. You already have, a million times over. You never left me, and that's all I could have ever asked for."

Chapter Twelve

PATTI

I threw an apron at Jake as soon as he walked through the door. "Where have you been?" I scooped the ice cream into the dish as the line continued to grow.

"Relax. I'm not late." Jake tied the apron behind him and pulled on some gloves.

"I've got this, go to the window and take some orders." I slid the cooler door closed and tore open the other. "What are you waiting for? The line isn't getting any shorter."

"Geez, it's only my second day." Jake stood at the counter and pulled open the window. "What am I supposed to do?" He turned to me and grinned. "What if I mess this up?" he whispered as the woman at the counter yelled her order through the window at him.

"Ask her to repeat the order. I'll take over once I get this order together." I scurried around the tiny room filling the dishes and juggling them to the window. I set them on the side and opened the pickup window. "Number twenty-six, your order is ready."

62

DEPENDING ON YOU

"Twenty-six?" Jake's eyes bugged out of his head. "It's only nine o'clock."

"I know." I wiped my hands on my apron. "That's why it would have been nice if you could have shown up an hour ago."

"But my schedule said nine."

"It said eight." I pointed to the wall. "We were both scheduled to come in for eight because it's a holiday."

"I didn't think Memorial Day counted." Jake shrugged and went back to taking orders. He closed the window and handed me the sheet.

"The parade didn't tip you off?" I pulled the cooler open and went back to filling bowls.

"I don't know. I guess I didn't think people would be eating ice cream as soon as they rolled out of bed." Jake walked around the cooler and watched me work.

"Well what else do they have to do in this shitty town?"

"Good point. I don't know how to make a shake. What am I supposed to do?" Jake held a cup in his hand and stood next to me.

"Oh my god, does your mother dress you, too?" I took the cup from him and started to make the shake. "As soon as this line dies down, I'm taking these things off the menu. It's too crazy to make a million different things today."

"You can do that?" Jake looked back at the window. "I don't think this line is going to go away any time soon."

"Well do something and help me get rid of them." I turned to the shake machine and turned it on, drowning out the buzz of voices coming through the window.

"I think that's the last of them." Jake wiped his arm across his brow.

"Yeah, until the parade is over, then they'll be back." I took

63

off my rubber gloves and sat on the counter. "I'm exhausted and it's not even ten."

"Me, too, and all I did was watch you." Jake laughed. "I'm sorry I wasn't much help. I'll try to figure things out for the next round."

"It's fine. They should have scheduled you a couple more times before this, but they knew I'd handle it, like always." I leaned my head on the wall. "So, what are your plans this weekend?"

"Like this weekend?" Jake wrinkled up his nose. "But today's Monday."

"I'm aware. The weekend coming up. You know, after we go back to school and leave for the day on Friday. What are you doing on the weekend?"

"I'm not sure. I think I've got to work." Jake ran his fingers through his hair before looking at the schedule on the wall. "Looks like we both have to work."

"Yeah, I know, but what are you doing after?" I rolled my eyes. "You're as exhausting as this place."

"Hey, that's not fair." He tossed a balled-up rag at me. "You didn't make yourself clear."

"Whatever." I shook my head. "I have no idea what Cate sees in you." I covered my mouth.

"What was that?" Jake raised his brow. "Cate likes me?" He touched his chest.

"I didn't say that." I hopped off the counter and took out an ice cream sandwich. "You must be hearing things."

"No, I heard you say Cate likes me." Jake reached in the cooler for a soda.

"That's not what I said." I took a bite and watched as he took a drink. "So, are you going to prom?"

64

DEPENDING ON YOU

"I don't know. I wasn't going to. I don't want to go alone. What's the fun in that?" Jake set his can down. "Unless you think I should ask Cate."

"You want to ask Cate to go to prom with you?" I finished off my snack and tossed the wrapper in the trash. "On one condition."

"What's that?" Jake pulled out a milkcrate and sat down.

"You get Andrew to ask me. We can go on a double date." I crossed my arms and tried to read his expression.

"You like Andrew?" Jake shook his head and laughed. "Really? What is it? His bushy curls or his face full of freckles?"

"That's mean. I thought he was your best friend."

"He is. I'm only teasing. What if I told you Andrew was going to ask you tomorrow?" Jake reached for his drink and tilted his head back to finish it.

"Shut up. He is not." I peeked out the window to make sure there wasn't a new line forming. "He's going to ask me to go to prom with him?"

"He is, but you better not tell him I said anything to you. He'll kick my ass."

"I won't say anything as long as you ask Cate to go with you." I held my hand out. "Deal?"

With a handshake we sealed the deal. "So, Cate likes me?" Jake's smile grew. "I can't believe the hottest girl at school likes me."

"If she wasn't my best friend, I'd kick your ass myself. But I'm glad you like her as much as she likes you." I looked at the calendar. "We've got to go dress shopping." I counted the days. "There's less than two weeks before prom."

"What do you think I'd look good in?" Jake put his hand on his hip and posed.

JESSICA AIKEN-HALL

"Pink ruffles. All the way to the floor." I tapped my finger on my lip. "And don't forget the glitter. Lots and lots of glitter."

"Oh, that sounds pretty." He spun around and stuck his butt in the air. "I can't wait to get all gussied up."

"Gussied up?" I raised my brow in disapproval. "Who are you, my grandma?"

"I don't know, is she hot?"

I threw the rag back at him. "Not as hot as Cate. Besides, you're not her type."

"Ouch." Jake laughed. "Are you sure she'll say yes? I can't stomach the rejection."

"Trust me, she'll say yes, probably before you even finish asking her. But if you tell her I said any of this I'll deny it all."

Jake held his hands up. "We already agreed to keep this between us."

"Good answer." I pushed my hand into his chest. "You better not hurt Cate."

"Why would I? I've had a crush on her since sixth grade." Jake took a step back. "I'm not a jerk."

I pointed my finger in his face. "Well, if you so much as make her shed one tear, I'm going to make you wish you were never born."

"I didn't think you were so mean." Jake looked down at his sneakers.

"I'm not, but when it comes to Cate, I'll do whatever it takes to make sure she's good. No one messes with her." I shrugged. "Don't do her wrong and I won't have to be mean."

"Understood." Jake put his hands in his pockets. "I like that you two are so close. I wish I had a friend like you."

"You have Andrew."

66

DEPENDING ON YOU

"Yeah, but we're nowhere near as close as the two of you. You're more like sisters than friends."

"That's because we are sisters. Blood sisters." I glanced over at the clock. "We better get ready for the mob. Are you ready for round two?"

"Aw, man. I had no idea dishing up ice cream was this stressful." Jake wiped the sweat off his hands. "I hate these things." The rubber glove ripped as he went to pull it on.

"Here, try these." I tossed him a box of a bigger size.

He held up a glove. "Seriously, you've had these all along and you made me cram myself into those tiny things? The more I get to know you, the more of a jerk I see you are."

I hit his chest. "Watch it, mister. Or I'll tell Cate you have herpes."

"Yeah, and I'm going to tell Andrew I gave them to you." He tossed the box at me.

"Yuck, you're disgusting." I stuck my tongue out at him.

"You started it." Jake put his hands on his hips.

"Truce?" I held my hand out for him.

He went to shake my hand and I pulled it away. "I don't know how Cate is friends with you." He dropped his hand.

I crossed my arms and gave him my meanest face. "I'm only teasing. I'm testing you. I want to see how much you can handle before you snap."

"It's going to take a lot more than that. I have three little sisters." Jake chuckled. "You've got nothing on those girls. They're little monsters."

"I didn't know you had little sisters." I smirked. "One more thing you and Cate have in common."

"I've seen her with hers. She seems way tamer than the

JESSICA AIKEN-HALL

demons I live with." Jake folded his hands in front of him. "I wasn't sure it was her sister. They don't look anything alike."

"That's rude. Who did you think it was?" I raised my brow.

"I don't know. I guess I thought she babysat or something." Jake shrugged. "I didn't mean to be rude."

"Ah, you're right, Sammy does look a lot different than Cate. But to be fair, Sammy is only three. She may change as she gets older."

"Three? One of my sister's is three. Does Sammy go to daycare or anything? Maybe our sisters know each other." Jake blew the hair out of his eyes.

"No, the only time she leaves the house is when Cate takes her places. She is more of a mother to Sammy than their mom." I bit my lip. "But anyway, maybe you can get the girls together. I'm sure Sammy would love someone her own age to play with."

"Yeah, that'd be fun, more time with the demon spawn." Jake dropped his head. "I shouldn't say that. It's not her fault her mother lets her get away with everything."

"Her mother? Isn't she your mother, too?" I slid my gloves on and opened the window.

"No, her mother is my stepmother. My mom died when I was little." Jake leaned on the counter. "Now don't you feel bad for being so mean to me?"

"Oh, Jake, I'm sorry. I had no idea." I hung my head. "I am a jerk."

"Nah, I was only kidding. About you being a jerk, not about my mom being dead." Nervous laughter filled the space between us. "Don't tell Cate, though. I don't want her to feel sorry for me."

"Okay." I nodded. "But you better tell her soon because we don't keep secrets from each other."

68

Chapter Thirteen

PATTI

"Hey guys. I didn't expect to see you here." Cate and Sammy were sitting with my mom on my front porch when I got home.

"Sorry." Cate stood up. "We can go if you want."

"What? Don't be crazy." I sat on the swing next to Mom and leaned my head on her shoulder. "I'm so tired."

"Long day?" Mom asked as she stroked my hair.

I kicked off my shoes. "Yes. We had over two hundred people there today. If I never see another bowl of ice cream, I'll be happy."

"Ice cream!" Sammy squealed.

"No, no ice cream." I sat up and reached my hand toward her tummy to tickle her.

She giggled as she inched away. "Ice cream."

"Sammy, knock it off," Cate snapped.

"It's okay, I was only kidding. It was a long day, that's all." I noticed the look on Cate's face and knew she had something she needed to tell me. "Mom, can you watch Sammy for a few minutes?"

69

JESSICA AIKEN-HALL

"Sure, we were about to go out back and start the grill." Mom stood up and took Sammy's hand. "You ready to help me make dinner?"

Sammy nodded as she skipped into the house with Mom.

"What's wrong?" I patted the seat next to me on the swing.

She paced the porch as she gnawed on her fingernail. "Nothing."

"Cate, come on, I know you better than that. What happened with your dad?" I stood up and stretched my arms over my head. "Come on, let's go inside."

She folded her arms and nodded. Her cheeks were tear-stained. "Alright."

I took her hand and led her to my room, closing the door behind us. "Spill it." I fell onto my bed and crossed my legs under me. "What's wrong?"

Cate took a deep breath and closed her eyes. "Mom's gone."

"Gone? What do you mean?"

"Dad said they got into a fight, and she packed her stuff and left." Cate paced in front of my bed. "He said they were taking a break."

"That's good, though, isn't it?" I hugged my pillow and leaned forward.

Cate shrugged. "I don't know. I mean, it is, but I don't know what to tell Sammy."

"Sammy's better off without her. You know that."

"I know. But she doesn't. She's going to take it personal. I mean, how can she not?" Cate sighed. "Now I'm trapped here forever."

"Not forever. Besides, you already knew you weren't going to leave her with your mom. This isn't really any different." I tilted my head and examined Cate. "What's really wrong?"

70

DEPENDING ON YOU

Cate started to cry. "I..." She covered her face with both hands.

I stood up and wrapped her in a hug. "What Cate?"

"I told Dad about what happened." She nuzzled her face into my neck and sobbed. "I didn't want him to know."

"Oh, Cate. I'm sorry." I tightened my arms around her. "But I'm glad you finally told him."

"He blamed himself. Now he feels like a failure. At being a dad and a husband." Cate sucked in air. "I shouldn't have told him."

"You should have. How is he supposed to keep you and Sammy safe if he didn't know?"

Cate pulled her head up and looked at me. "That's what he said."

"See, it's a good thing he knows." I pushed the hair behind her ear. "I'm so glad you don't have to carry that secret any longer. I'm proud of you."

"If it was such a good thing to do, then why does it feel so bad?" Cate rubbed her nose and sat on my bed.

"Because it's hard to talk about. It brings it all back to life. But the sooner you get it out in the open, the sooner you can heal."

Cate sniffled. "Why are you so smart?"

"I'm not." I laughed. "But I am the granter of wishes."

"Granter of wishes?" Cate scrunched up her nose. "What are you talking about?"

"I'm not supposed to say." I covered my face and peeked at her through my open fingers.

"Well now you have to." Curiosity replaced her sadness as she waited for me to answer.

71

"Okay, but only if you promise not to get mad." I pressed my teeth together and smiled.

"Come on, Patti, tell me. I can't take the suspense."

"We're going to prom." The grin spread across my face. "Jake is going to ask you tomorrow, and Andrew is going to ask me."

"Are you serious? You aren't making him ask me, are you? He's not doing it out of pity is he?" Cate rubbed her forehead.

"No, he likes you. I asked him if he was going to prom, and he said no. So, I asked him why not, and he said because he didn't have anyone to go with. And then I asked him who he wanted to ask, and he said you."

"You, like you? Or you like me?" Cate pointed at me.

"You like Cate, you." I wiggled my eyebrows. "So, then I asked him who Andrew was taking and he said Andrew is going to ask me tomorrow."

"Really? They like us, too?" Cate's smile grew. "So, we're going to the prom together?"

"Yeah, it's going to be perfect." I leaned over and hugged Cate. "We're going to have the best summer ever. Just like we planned."

"But if he finds out about my mom, he probably won't want to take me." Cate frowned. "Who wants to date a girl who can't even make her mom love her?"

"Don't be dumb. Your mom's a bitch. The important people love you. Jake's a decent guy, he's not going to judge you based on your lunatic mother."

"How do you know that? I come with a lot of baggage. I'm sure he doesn't want to deal with all my drama." Cate hung her head as sadness crept back in.

DEPENDING ON YOU

"He has his own drama. We all do. No one has a perfect life. The people who say they don't are lying."

"What kind of drama could he possible have?" Cate shook her head. "It's a waste of time."

"Did you know his mom died when he was little?" I covered my mouth to try to take back the secret I was in charge of holding. "I wasn't supposed to say that."

"She did? When?" Cate asked.

"I don't know, he didn't say, but he has a miserable stepmother and three younger demon sisters." I sighed. "He didn't want you to know because he didn't want you to feel sorry for him. I promised not to tell you yet. He said he was going to tell you."

"I had no idea." Cate laid on the bed and stared at the ceiling. "He's never even mentioned his sisters."

"He doesn't like them. I know, it sounds worse than it is." I held my hand up. "He said his stepmother lets them get away with everything, so they're little demons. One is Sammy's age, though, so I tried to set up a playdate."

"You didn't." Cate covered her head with the pillow. "You're just the queen of match making." She laughed. "I can't believe you."

"What? I thought it would be good for Sammy to have some friends her own age. My mom's cool and all, but Sammy's three, she should have friends who will sit in the sandbox with her."

"Your mom would if Sammy asked." The smile returned to Cate's face. "Sammy's lucky to have your mom. So am I."

"Me, too." I put my head on Cate's chest. "We've got to go dress shopping."

"I still can't believe you set that all up."

73

JESSICA AIKEN-HALL

"I didn't do anything, it was already in the works." I looked up at Cate. "You're going to be stunning in your gown. We're going to make it be the best day ever."

"It will be one of the first best days ever of the summer." Cate held up her hand. "1998 is going to be a year to remember."

Chapter Fourteen

CATE

The dress fell to the floor around my feet. "Ugh! I'll never find one that works."

"That's not true. The last two you had on were perfect." Patti leaned on the dressing room door. "Come on, pick one already."

"It's useless. There's no way I'm going to the prom in any of these." I pulled at my hair and looked into my bloodshot eyes. "Just go without me."

"No, if you're not going, then neither am I." Patti knocked on the door. "Let me in." She turned the knob.

"Don't be ridiculous. You have to go. That's not fair to Andrew." I opened the door and saw the dress Patti was holding. "There's no way I'm trying that thing on."

Patti pushed the lavender dress into my arms. "Please? For me?"

"Fine, if I have to." I stepped into the gown and turned so Patti could zip it up.

"Oh my god, Cate, it's beautiful." She straightened out the front and took a step back.

75

'I doubt it." I crossed my arms to cover as much of myself as possible.

'See for yourself." She spun me around until I faced the mirror.

"Wow." I did a half turn and watched the dress fall around my hips. 'It's perfect."

'See, I told you." Patti put her arm around my shoulder. 'Look at us. We're going to be the best dressed girls there."

"Where did you find this? I searched every rack." I twirled around.

'It was on the rack, but you thought it was ugly." Patti giggled. "You didn't want to try it on, but I made you. You're so beautiful." She kissed my cheek. 'Jake is a lucky guy."

'I hope so." I covered my mouth to catch the laughter.

'One thing at a time, grasshopper." Patti smoothed out her gown. 'I love this color. We look like princesses."

"We do." I admired our reflection in the mirror. "Teal is your color. It brings out my eyes." I batted my eyes.

"You're a fool." She tapped my stomach. 'I hope that's not all it brings out." She winked.

'Now who's getting ahead of herself?" We both balled over in laughter. 'I can't wait for prom night."

'It's less than two weeks away." Patti pulled up her dress. 'Looks like I need to shave my legs."

'Me, too, but I'm going to wait until that morning, so I don't get all prickly." I wrinkled my nose. 'I wish it was normal for girls to be hairy. I hate shaving."

'I know, but it makes me feel so much sexier when my legs are smooth." Patti let her dress fall back into place. 'Let's get changed and get out of here."

When I took the dress off I noticed the tag was missing. I

DEPENDING ON YOU

searched the tiny dressing room, picking up everything. I couldn't find it anywhere. My face flushed at the thought of having to leave it behind. I'd never be able to find another dress that worked as well. "Patti? Hey, do you have the tag?" She didn't answer me. I put my clothes back on so I could broaden the search.

"Patti? Are you still in there?" When I knocked on the door it swung open. Patti wasn't in there, but her clothes were. I went back out into the store and saw Patti tucking something back into her purse. "I couldn't find the tag. I don't even know if I can afford this thing." The dress was draped over my arms.

"Let me see it." Patti reached for it and handed it to the cashier.

"What are you doing?" I watched as the woman handed her a bag.

"Happy birthday." Patti smiled. "Mom wanted to buy us our dresses for an early birthday gift."

"I can't accept that." I followed Patti back to the changing room. "How much was it? I can pay for it."

She closed the door between us. "No, Mom gave me specific orders to pay for both of our dresses. She wanted us to pick ones we loved without worrying about the cost."

"Patti, that's nuts. I can't accept it." I held up the dress to look at it one more time before I put it in the bag. "At least let me know how much it is."

"Nope, Mom made me promise not to talk about the cost." She walked out of the room with her dress neatly folded. "Let me put this in there." She carefully put her dress on top of mine. "Let's go give Mom a fashion show." Patti took my hand. "Please don't make a big deal out of this. She really wanted us to have fun. It's important to her."

77

"Okay." I couldn't find the right words. I was grateful, but there was nothing I could say to express my gratitude. Being loved like a daughter by someone who wasn't even my mom was a mixture of nice and devastating. I wished my mom was as invested in me as Mrs. Thomas was.

"Good." She swung our hands as we walked out of the store. "This is going to be so much fun."

"I know. I don't know how I'm going to sleep the next few nights."

"Try. You'll look like shit with bags under your eyes." Patti shrugged. "I guess we could always cake the concealer on."

"We will anyway, along with the mascara and eye liner." I laughed. "Do you remember when we first started wearing makeup?"

"Oh god, don't remind me. That was terrible." She covered her face. "I can't believe we left the house looking like that."

"I can't believe your mom let us." I shook my head as I pulled up images of Patti and me with clown makeup on. "It was like Halloween; except we were the only two with costumes on."

Patti snorted. "We were amateurs."

"Aren't we still?"

"No, we've come a long way since seventh grade." Patti stopped to look at me. "We're model material now." She framed her hands around her face. "Let's strike a pose."

"Never do that again." I rolled my eyes. "If we're going to pretend we're cool, we can't do that kind of stuff, at least not where everyone can see us."

Patti tugged on my arm. "Do you want to go show our friends our dresses?"

DEPENDING ON YOU

"I thought you were too freaked out to go back in there." I glanced across the street to the sea of granite stones.

"No, I was only teasing." I pulled on my hand as we crossed the road.

Calmness fell around me as my feet hit the ground. "Let's go to our spot." I inhaled the scent of moss and lilacs as I walked up the path to the back of the cemetery. "We should bring the guys here."

Patti was a few steps behind me, her eyes on the path. "No, I don't want to share this place with anyone else." Patti panted. "I forgot how steep this hill is."

"We're almost there." I turned and took her hand to pull her the rest of the way up. At the top, I set the bag down and took in the view. "This is heaven."

Patti snickered. "As close as we're going to get to it."

"At least for now." I lifted my chin to the sky and let the sun cascade down over me. "This is the best spot in Lawrenceville."

"It doesn't take much." Patti put her hand around my waist. "When I get back from college, we can build that house we always talked about."

"I thought you forgot about that." I turned to look at the open field behind us. "It's the perfect spot. You'll never find neighbors any quieter." I sat on the grass and held my knees. "It's crazy how good this place makes me feel."

Patti joined me on the ground. "Not really, we've spent a lot of time here. Once you get past the creepiness of it all, it's actually breathtaking."

"It was never creepy for me." I plucked at blades of grass until I had a handful. "It's always been comforting. I feel heard here. My voice gets absorbed, and what I say matters. I don't feel like that any place else."

79

"I'm sorry, Cate. I didn't know I was such an awful friend."
Patti stared into the distance. "I should have..."

"What are you talking about? You're part of this place. I was
talking about you, too. You're the best friend a girl could have.
A once in a lifetime friend." I tossed the grass at her. "Why
would you even think I was talking about you?"

Patti's shoulders fell. "I don't know. I guess I just feel like
I'm letting you down by leaving. I should stay here and build
my life with you. And my mom." She shook her head. "If I were
a good person, how could I even think about leaving her alone?
Dad's only been gone a year. This wasn't how it was supposed
to be."

"That's not true. You're going on a grand adventure so you
can build the life you deserve. There's nothing here for any of
us. You have so much to offer the world. Think about all of the
kids you're going to be helping." I stood up and held my arms
out. "You're meant for bigger and better things than staying
here. Don't let guilt turn you into a prisoner."

Patti wiped the tears off her cheeks. "I'm going to miss you
so damn much."

"No, you won't." I poked her in the chest. "Because I'll
always be right there with you." I held my pinky up. "Together
forever."

Patti wrapped her pinky with mine. "And ever."

Chapter Fifteen
CATE

"Go on, girls, blow out the candles." Mrs. Thomas hovered over us as we held hands and closed our eyes. "Don't forget to make a wish."

Patti and I shared a secret smile before closing our eyes to make our wish. The one we couldn't speak of.

"You better have wished what I think you did." Patti grabbed my hand and squeezed as she wiggled her eyebrows.

I covered my mouth to hide the growing smile and nodded. "It's the final countdown." My face flushed when I noticed Mrs. Thomas holding the knife over the cake.

"I don't even want to know, do I?" Mrs. Thomas shook her head before making the first cut.

Patti snorted. "Oh, Mom, get your head out of the gutter. We just want to go to a concert before we go off to school."

Mrs. Thomas raised her brow. "Uh huh." She handed me a slice of chocolate cake with strawberry frosting. "You girls seem to forget my bedroom is right next to yours." She pointed to her ear. "I hear *everything*." Her eyes looked away as mine went to

81

my cake. "Just don't do anything stupid. You're too smart for that."

A tear rolled down my cheek as I closed my eyes in an attempt to hold the emotion in.

"What's the matter, honey? Is everything alright?" Mrs. Thomas licked the pink frosting off her finger before coming over to me.

I nodded. "Yeah." With a deep breath I closed my eyes. "You remembered."

She moved the hair out of my face and kneeled to wrap her arms around me. "Of course, I did. I love you Cate." She kissed the top of my head. "It was Patti's idea."

Patti put her arm around me. "It was your turn for your favorite. Besides, it's growing on me." Her lips curled up when she took a bite.

"Thank you." I wiped my check dry. "For everything."

"Oh, Cate, you don't have to thank me. It's what you do when you're family." Mrs. Thomas went back over to the cake and continued serving the rest of the guests.

"I'm going to miss this," I whispered as I looked over at Patti.

"What are you talking about? This isn't the end of anything. We'll still celebrate our birthdays together." She held up her fork before shoving it into her mouth.

"We better." I savored the flavors as they mixed in my mouth. Mrs. Thomas was a great cook, although I didn't have any real comparison.

Patti wiped her mouth with her napkin and nodded her head toward the backyard. "Come on, let's go get some fresh air."

I glanced around the room. It appeared everyone else was

82

DEPENDING ON YOU

lost in their own conversations. I slipped out of my chair and pushed it in before following Patti outside. She took my hand and dragged me to the edge of the lawn. Tall pine trees stood before us. "We haven't been out there in ages."

"I know. That's why it's perfect." Patti tugged me through the tall grass and pricker bushes. "Come see what I did."

At the base of the treehouse a flood of memories washed over me. My heart stopped as they crashed around me. With my hand on the trunk, I was transported back in time. "I can't believe it's been so long."

"Think about all of the wasted opportunities." Patti turned her head to look at me as she climbed up the ladder. "Come on up. I want to show you what I've done."

As my feet stood on the crooked boards we nailed on here so many years ago, I became that seven-year-old little girl again. A wave of panic prevented me from moving. There was no way up or down. Frozen in place, the sweat beaded on my forehead.

Patti reached her hand out the door. "It's okay, Cate, I've got you." She inched closer to me. "You're safe now. You're not that little girl anymore."

I looked up at Patti and took her hand. "I'm sorry. I didn't expect this to..."

"Don't be sorry." Patti helped pull me into the treehouse. "I'm sorry. I didn't even think about how this might be weird for you."

As my heartrate began to slow down, I looked around the tiny space. "You've been busy."

"It's your... our birthday surprise." Patti stretched her arms out as she spun around, her hands bumping into the walls. "Do you like it?"

83

"It's great." My brow furrowed. "But why?" I cleared my throat. "I mean, why now, right before you're leaving?"

Patti snickered as she twisted her flipflop on the floor. "It's our very own love shack."

"Oh my god, Patti." I shook my head. "In here?"

She flopped down on a freshly made cot and pulled back the cover before running her hands over the satin sheets. "I think it'll be romantic."

"We have different ideas about the definition of that word." I laughed as I crawled across the uneven floor and joined her on the cot. "Hmm, it is cozy."

"See." Patti rested her head on my chest. "It's the perfect place. No one will even know we're out here."

"I guess it's better than the backseat." I played with Patti's hair as she snuggled into me.

"I wanted to make sure our first time was special. Something to remember. This place can always be ready, in case... you know."

"Are you sure you're ready? Maybe we're being immature about this whole thing. Maybe the man of your dreams is waiting for you in New Jersey."

"I'm ready. You don't have to do it if you're not." Patti pulled her head off my chest to look at me. "I also thought this could be a good place for you to get away if things get too bad at home."

"You didn't have to go through all this trouble for me. I'll be all right." I bit my bottom lip and closed my eyes. Memories of our first time in the treehouse raced through my head.

Patti placed her hand on mine. "Take a deep breath and let it go."

"I can't believe you hid me out here for almost a week." I

DEPENDING ON YOU

blinked away the tears. "You were an accessory in a kidnapping case."

"It was my job to keep you safe. So, that's what I did." Patti lifted her shoulders. "No one knew where you were."

"I know. This was the best hide out. A little spooky when the owls landed in the tree over there." I pointed out the tiny window.

"I should have brought you inside when my parents went to bed." Patti blew out a puff of air. "It was pretty lousy of me to leave you out here all alone."

"If you brought me in, your parents would have called mine. Staying out here was my only option." I rubbed my finger over the nail. "At least you let me keep the lantern out here."

"Thank God I thought of that. It gets so dark in here." Patti looked around the treehouse. "I never stayed out here overnight alone before. It must have been terrifying."

"It was a lot less scary than being at home. My mom never even told my dad I was missing. She told him I was at my grandma's house. I could have been dead for all she knew." I scrunched up my nose. "She's an awful person."

"You're the bravest girl I know." Patti twirled a lock of my hair around her finger. "I'm so glad you came to me for help."

"You're pretty brave yourself. How many seven-year-olds would know how to hide someone? You even brought me food and drinks." I laughed. "And toilet paper."

"Have you ever wiped your butt with leaves?" Patti held her hand up. "It's horrible."

"No, can't say that I have, thanks to you." I put my hand on Patti's shoulder. "How can I ever repay you for all you have done for me? I haven't been half the friend to you that you've been to me."

85

"Don't be crazy. You're the best friend a girl could ask for. Just by being you. I was lucky I never needed you to rescue me from my family, but you rescued me from myself plenty of times."

"How?" I squinted my eyes. "You didn't need to be rescued."

"Yes, I did." Patti nodded. "Before we met, I didn't think I'd ever find a friend. If you haven't noticed, I'm not like the other kids."

"We met in second grade. How do you know you wouldn't have made other friends if I wasn't around?"

Patti shrugged. "I just know. You were meant for me."

"And I was meant for you." I wrapped my arms around her. "Well, I'm glad everyone else was too dumb to notice a good thing when it was right in front of them."

"Now I want to listen to Jewel." Patti snorted. "I hope Andrew gets to see the inside of this place, if you know what I mean."

"Are you talking about the treehouse, or?"

"You're such a pervert." Patti buried her head in the cot. "Let's leave it at the treehouse for now. I don't think I'm ready for anyone to see inside there yet."

"We should get back to the party before someone finds us out here." I stood up and pulled Patti to her feet. "Thanks for turning this place into such an awesome love shack."

"Anything for you." Patti kissed my cheek. "Love you to the cemetery and back."

"I don't think that means what you think it does." I crossed my arms and laughed. "Till death do us part."

Chapter Sixteen

PATTI

"Why are you knocking? Just come in," I yelled from the bathroom. Two more taps. "What are you doing?"

"Hi, Patti." Mr. Silver took his hat off and lowered his head.

"Hey, Mr. Silver, sorry. I was expecting Cate." I pulled my robe closed. "Is everything alright?"

"Can I come in?" His bloodshot eyes looked vacant.

I peered around him, looking for Cate. "Sure."

He cleared his throat. "Is your mom here?"

"No, she's out picking up some lunch." I folded my arms tight. "What's the matter? You look like you've been crying."

He nodded. "That's because I have." He looked through me. "Can we sit down?"

I backed up into the living room. "Where's Cate? Is she okay?" My pulse pounded in my neck as I awaited his answer.

"I don't know where she is. I haven't been home yet." Mr. Silver rubbed his hand over his worn face. "I still need to pick Sammy up from daycare."

"Do you need me to go get her?"

87

JESSICA AIKEN-HALL

"No, I will." He blew out his breath. "I know tonight's the prom and I don't want to ruin it for you girls, but..." He rubbed his hands on his pants.

"But what?" The anticipation was the only thing keeping me from totally freaking out.

"Mrs. Silver isn't with us anymore."

"Yeah, I know. Cate told me. She already knows." I tilted my head and tried to make sense of it all.

"No, I mean, she died." He hung his head. "I uh, wanted to tell you before Cate, so you'd be able to help her through it. I was hoping your mom was here so I could talk to her about it."

My mouth fell open. "How?"

"It's too early to tell, but it looks like it was an overdose." He leaned his head back. "I'm not going to tell Cate until tomorrow. I don't want it to get in her way tonight. I just don't know how long it will be before it's on the radio."

"I'm sorry Mr. Silver. I promise I won't tell her, and I'll make sure we don't turn the radio on tonight." I covered my mouth. "I can't believe this."

"I know. I wasn't expecting it, either." He put his hands on his knees. "I shouldn't have told you all this." He stood up and put his hand on my back. "I'm sorry. I should have waited."

"No, it's fine, Mr. Silver. I'll make sure Cate doesn't find out tonight. I'll make sure she has the best day ever." I walked him to the door.

"But you're just a kid. I shouldn't have made you carry this around. Not tonight of all nights." He put his hat on. "I'm sorry. I didn't want anything to mess tonight up for Cate, I wasn't even thinking about what I just did to you."

"It's fine. Really. I'll take care of it." I held the door open as I waited for him to leave.

88

DEPENDING ON YOU

He took his hat back off and ran his fingers through his hair. "Do you think you could come over tomorrow sometime? I'd like you to be there when I tell the girls."

"Of course." I nodded. "You better get out of here before Cate shows up."

"You're right." He tipped his hat. "Thanks, Patti. Please try to forget about it tonight and have a great time. You two deserve to have the best night of your lives."

"We will, Mr. Silver." I watched him back out of the driveway before I shut the door. I fell onto the couch and tried to push it all out of my head. I didn't want to keep any secrets from Cate, especially not something as important as this one. I leaned forward and cradled my head in my hands. Thoughts of my dad weaved in and out, bringing the tears I didn't want to shed tonight. I didn't want to think about him not being here to see me in my dress or leaving with my date. He was supposed to be here, just like Cate's mom should have been.

I shook the thoughts out of my head and screamed. "Not tonight. Not tonight." I pulled at my hair. "Get out of my head."

"Honey, are you alright?" Mom set the bag down on the coffee table before sitting beside me.

I fell into her arms and sobbed. "No."

She rubbed my back, extenuating the sadness I was so desperately trying to swallow. "Oh honey. Don't be sad. Tonight is going to be magical. You and Cate get to be princesses. Forget about everything else and make some new memories."

I nodded as she held me. "I miss Dad."

"So do I." She pushed the hair away from my face. "He's here with us. I know he's going to be watching over you

89

tonight. He is so proud of you. Don't ever doubt it. He will always be with you."

"I'm sorry. I didn't mean to..."

"Don't be sorry. I knew this was going to be hard. It's the first big night that he's not here. It's okay to cry, Patti. You don't always have to be tough."

"I know. I didn't want to make you sad."

She wiped the tears off my cheek. "Don't try to protect me. That's my job. I know how bad it hurts. I want you to talk to me, tell me how you're doing. Don't do this on your own. If we talk about our feelings, maybe it will be easier for both of us."

I rubbed my eyes. "I don't know where Cate is."

"I'm sure she'll be here soon. I know she's as excited as you are." Mom picked up the bag. "Let's go eat while we wait for Cate."

"I wish she'd hurry up and get here." I pulled the curtain back and saw Mr. Silver's car pull into the driveway. I swallowed the dread that was creeping into my throat as I waited for him to get out. When the door opened, Cate got out. Relief flushed away the fear. "She's here." I raced to the door.

"Hey, sorry I'm late. I was waiting to hear back from my dad. He said I could use his car tonight." She got her bag and rushed up the walkway.

"I thought we were riding with the guys." I took the bag from her as she took off her shoes.

"We were, but I thought you and Andrew could ride together and Jake and I could in my dad's car."

I held my finger to my lips and nodded my head toward the kitchen. "Mom picked us up some lunch. She thought we should try to eat something before we go in case we get too nervous to eat later."

90

DEPENDING ON YOU

"That's a good idea." Cate rubbed her belly. "I am starving."

"You girls think I'm an old lady, but I remember my prom." She pulled out a chair and sat down. "I was a ball of nerves. I wanted everything to be perfect." She took a bite of her sandwich and covered her mouth while she chewed. "Tonight will be one of those nights you remember forever."

"If it's so special how come I've never heard you talk about it before?" I picked up half of my turkey sandwich.

"Well, that's because I went with Sid." Mom dabbed at her mouth with her napkin.

"Sid? Who's that?" I asked before crunching into a chip.

"He was my boyfriend senior year. We didn't last much longer than that night, but I didn't mention him because I didn't want to make your father jealous." Mom smiled. "I met your dad that night, too."

"You met Dad at your prom?"

"I did. He was part of the band." Mom's smile grew. "Sid wasn't too pleased with me when he saw your dad and I talking by the punch bowl." She giggled. "Your father handed me a napkin with his phone number on it."

"Wait, Dad was in a band?" I twisted my mouth. "How come I never knew that?"

"Because he wasn't really in the band. He was friends with one of the guys and his job was to set up and tear down. He was a good man, but he did not have one musical bone in his body." Mom leaned on the table. "See, this is what I mean. Go tonight with an open mind and heart. Magic happens when you aren't looking for it."

"So maybe we'll find our husbands tonight." Cate took a drink of her soda and burped. "I won't if I keep that up."

91

JESSICA AIKEN-HALL

"Mr. Right won't care if you burp. He'll love you just the same. True love is deeper than that." Mom pushed herself away from the table. "I'm so excited to see my two princesses."

"I don't know if we'll morph into royalty when we zip up our gowns, but we'll do our best." I laughed as I stuffed the last of my sandwich into my mouth.

"Speak for yourself. I fully intend to be a princess tonight." Cate held up her necklace. "This was my grandma's. Dad gave it to me for my birthday. He said it was her favorite."

"Wow, Cate, that's beautiful." Mom bent down to examine the ruby hanging from the gold chain.

"It was her birthstone." Cate's face glowed. "I've been eyeing this thing since I was little."

"What a sweet gift." Mom went back to the sink to clean up.

"He said when I get married, he'll give me the rest of her jewelry." Cate looked down at the gem around her neck. "Who knows, maybe I'll get them sooner than later."

"In good time. Don't rush into anything you're not ready for." Mom cleared her throat. "I know what usually happens on prom night."

"Mom." I covered my eyes.

"What? I don't want to be a grandmother yet." She wiped her hands off and handed me a box. "I'm not encouraging you to use these, but I want you to have them just in case."

My cheeks heated a hundred degrees. "Oh my god, Mom."

"What? You're both adults. I know what happens on prom night." She winked.

"Gross, Mom." I stuck my tongue out. "Now I definitely won't need these."

Mom shrugged. "Well, it's better to be safe than sorry."

Chapter Seventeen
CATE

Celine Dion sang the last song of the night. Patti and Andrew and Jake and I danced together in a tight circle as *Because You Loved Me* finished off our senior prom. With my head rested on Jake's shoulder I knew that I was ready. He didn't pull away when the music stopped, or when the lights started coming back on. "I don't want this night to end," he whispered in my ear.

"It doesn't have to." I kissed his neck. "Let's go somewhere quiet, just the two of us."

"What about them?" Jake motioned to Patti and Andrew who were sitting at the table waiting for us.

"We can ask them." I took his hand and walked over to Patti. "Come to the bathroom with me." I dropped Jake's hand and took hers.

She grabbed her purse off the table and followed me. "I'm kind of tired." Patti yawned. "I think I'm going to see if Andrew will take me home."

"You don't want to stay out with him?" I leaned into the

93

mirror and rubbed the eyeliner, pushing it back in place. "We were thinking we could find a place and hang out. Don't you want to come?"

"No, I don't think I like Andrew." Patti crossed her arms. "Not like I thought."

"Really? It looked like you two were having a good time." I looked at her reflection in the mirror.

"We did. I don't think I'm ready. Not tonight anyway." She reached into her purse and handed me a couple of the condoms her mom gave us. "In case you need these."

I let them hang in the air between us. "No, I should go home with you. We came together, we should leave together."

"Don't be crazy. Take them. I know you want to." Patti smiled. "We don't have to leave together. Go make some memories."

"I shouldn't. Not without you." I took the condoms out of her hand. "I'm a terrible friend."

"No, you're not. This is what you've been waiting for." Patti put her arm around me. "You can tell me all about it in the morning."

"I really like him. He's even better than I had imagined." I lifted my shoulders as my smile grew. "I think I love him."

"Well, then, you know what you need to do." Patti took my hands and looked into my eyes. "Have the time of your life. Don't let anything get in your way tonight. All of the problems can wait until morning." Her eyes darted away.

"What are you talking about?"

"Nothing." She put her arms around my neck and kissed my cheek. "Have a great time. I love you, Cate."

"I love you, too. You're sure you're not mad at me?"

DEPENDING ON YOU

"No, not at all." She yawned. "Why don't you use the tree house? It's all ready for you."

"Yeah? Are you sure it's okay?" I tucked the condoms into my bra.

"That's what I did it for. My mom will be sleeping, so you can park in the driveway. She'll never suspect a thing." She covered my mouth to catch another yawn. "I'll see you in the morning."

I took her hand and squeezed. "I can't believe it's happening."

"Enjoy every moment." Patti kissed my cheek.

Andrew and Jake were still at the table drinking the rest of their sodas and sharing jokes. "I thought you guys ran off without us." Andrew stood up and stretched.

"No, we wouldn't do that." Patti smiled and took his hand. "Let's get out of here."

The four of us walked to the parking lot together. I handed Jake my keys. "Good night, guys." I blew kisses to Patti as she got into Andrew's car.

"Good night?" Jake scratched his head. "I thought we were all hanging out."

"No, just the two of us." I winked. "Come, on let's go." Jake opened the door for me and raced around to the driver's side.

"Are you sure your dad is okay with me driving his car?" Jake put the key in the ignition and looked over at me. "I don't want to do anything to piss him off."

"Don't worry about him." I leaned over and kissed him. "Let's get out of here."

Jake backed the car out of the space and honked the horn at

95

Andrew and Patti. "I rented a room at the Hillside Inn." He reached over for my hand.

"You rented a room? Were you planning this the whole time?"

"No, I didn't know. I mean, I wanted tonight to be perfect, so I did everything I could think of to make it that way." He cleared his throat. "It's stupid. I'm sorry. We don't have to go if you don't want to."

"For the whole night?" I fidgeted in my seat. "I don't think I can stay out all night."

"Yeah, of course. I probably shouldn't stay out all night, either. We don't want the cops to come looking for us." He laughed.

"Right, that's not how I want you to meet my dad."

"Oh my god, that's right." Jake tapped his fingers on the steering wheel. "I'm kidnapping a cop's daughter in his stolen car."

"Sounds even more exciting when you say it out loud." I inched closer to him and put my hand on his thigh.

Jake squirmed in his seat. "Are you sure you want to go?"

"Yes." I leaned over and kissed his neck, biting his ear.

Jake put both hands on the wheel to turn into the parking lot. "You're going to get us into an accident." He put the car into park and kissed me. "Do you want to go see our room?" He got out of the car and held my door open, giving me his hand to help me out.

"Aren't you a gentleman." With my hand in his I followed him to the door in front of us.

He pulled the key out of his pocket and pushed the door open. The bed was covered in rose petals and a bottle of cham-

DEPENDING ON YOU

pagne was in a bucket of ice on the table. He closed the door behind us, locking both the locks. "What do you think?" He tossed the key on the nightstand.

"You did all of this for me?" I set my purse down and kicked off my shoes. "You're even sweeter than I thought."

Jake pulled off his tie. "I wanted to give you a night you would remember."

I walked over to him and put my hands on his face as I guided his mouth to mine. "It's perfect, just like you."

We made love in comfort and luxury and held each other as the hours slipped away too fast. "Cate." Jake kissed my forehead. "Don't you think we should get going? I'd love to stay here all night with you, but I don't want to give your dad a reason to hate me."

I looked up and kissed him. "I don't want to leave you. I want to stay."

"I know, but I want to be able to see you again. I don't want to press my luck." The warmth of his hand on my back wasn't something I wanted to be without.

"You're probably right." I kissed him once more before sitting up, holding the sheet over my naked body.

He drove me to his house where we spent ten minutes kissing goodbye. I got out of the car to drive myself home and wrapped my arms around him, giving him one more kiss. "Thank you for everything. It was the best night of my life."

"No, thank you. It was better than I could have imagined." He leaned in through the open window to kiss me. "I'll call you later."

My body replayed all of the sensations of the night as I made the drive home in the wee hours of the night. The

97

JESSICA AIKEN-HALL

driveway was empty when I pulled in. Dad must have had to work the late shift. Where's Sammy? My heart sank at the thought of her home alone. Was I supposed to be home earlier to take care of her? I raced out of the car and into the house.

"Sammy? Sammy? Where are you?" I flipped on all the lights and searched through the entire house. Her bed was empty, and so was Dad's. In the kitchen I saw a note on the table. "Had to work late, be back in the morning. Sammy is with Patti's mom. Have a good night. Love you. Dad."

I sat at the table and reread the note and snickered. "Thank god for the Hillside Inn." There was no way Mrs. Thomas would have been sleeping when we would have showed up and seeing Sammy would have killed the mood. I stretched my arms over my head and yawned.

In my room, I slipped on my sweats and a T-shirt and climbed into bed. Now that I knew Sammy was safe, I could get some sleep. As soon as my eyes closed, the ringing of the phone broke the silence. I sprung out of bed and ran to get the phone in the kitchen. "Hello?"

"Cate?" Her voice was almost unrecognizable. "I need you."

"Patti? Is that you?" I twisted the phone cord around my finger.

"Yeah, I need you to come. Now."

"Where are you? What's wrong?" My heart raced as her panic became mine.

"Meet me at our place." As soon as she hung up the phone, I got the keys and flew out the door. Patti had never needed me, not like this. I was always the one who needed her. It was my turn to fix whatever needed fixing.

I slammed the car in reverse and peeled out of the driveway. I slid Tracy Chapman's CD into the stereo and tried to let her voice cover me in calmness. I raced to our place as my heart pounded in my chest. There was no time to think about what was happening, or why Patti needed me. The only way to fix it was to get there. With my foot pressed to the floor I turned into the gate at the cemetery. The back end of my car swung around. I slowed down enough to gain control. At the bottom of the hill, I hit the gas and accelerated to the top.

I turned the volume up to try to drown out the fear. I sang *Fast Car* as my speed increased. At the crest of the hill my car struck something. I gave it more gas to see if I could clear whatever was in my way. Whatever was under me was not going to stop me. I needed to get to Patti.

I opened the door and ran to the field. Patti was sitting on the ground with her arms around her knees. I ran to her side and put my arm around her, pulling her close to me. "Oh, Patti. I got here as fast as I could. What's the matter? What happened?"

"We need to get out of here." Her voice shook as much as her body.

"Okay, let's go." I stood up and put my arm around her. The sun hadn't come up yet, but I could see that her dress had been torn and was dirty. When we got to the car, I screamed. "Oh my god. Oh my god."

"Get in the car. We need to get out of here." Patti ran to the passenger's side and slammed the door shut.

"Oh my god." I pulled at my hair and screamed. My fists balled up at my sides, I paced in front of the car. The thing I hit was a man. A dead man.

"Get in the car. We need to get out of here!" Patti yelled through my open door.

"I can't leave him here." I got on my knees and tried to see what I had done. "I need to call the police."

"No, Cate. We need to get out of here. Now, Cate." Patti rushed over to me and pulled me up. "Get in the damn car."

"Maybe he'll be okay if I get him some help." I covered my face. "Oh my god, what have I done?"

"Get in, Cate." The harshness of Patti's voice made me do as she said.

My hands shook as I put the car in reverse. "I don't want to hit him again."

"Why? He's already dead." Patti scanned the area. "Turn around right there and don't look back."

Back on the path, I could see the lump of the man on the ground in my rearview mirror. "I need to find my dad."

Patti grabbed my arm. "No. You can't tell anyone about this. We're eighteen now, we could go to jail. This has to be our secret."

"It was an accident. They'll understand." The man had disappeared out of sight. "I really think I need to tell someone."

"God damn it, Cate. No. You can't tell anyone. Neither one of us can. Do you understand me?" Her nails dug into my arm.

I pulled the car over at the end of the path. "Okay, I won't tell."

"Promise me, this stays between us."

"I promise." Darkness was pulled away by the rising sun. "What happened to you?" The dirt and blood on Patti's dress was now unable to be hidden by the night.

"Nothing. Don't worry about me. We need to get out of here." Patti sunk into her seat. "Can you bring me to your house?"

DEPENDING ON YOU

"Sure." I glanced over and saw the stoic look on her face. "Do you want to talk about it?"

"No, I just need a shower."

"Okay. Dad's working and Sammy's with your mom, so we have the house to ourselves for a little while." The rest of the drive home was pained with silence. I knew there was something she wasn't telling me, but I had enough of my own problems to worry about now. I just killed a man.

Chapter Eighteen

PATTI

I couldn't get the water hot enough. I needed to wash away everything I couldn't talk about. Never to be spoken of again. I rubbed the Dove soap over my body until my skin was raw. I didn't want any evidence of what happened anywhere near me. With a hand full of shampoo, I lathered my hair, washing the soap and memories away.

I bit the inside of my hand and screamed, trying to mask the sound. I didn't want Cate to hear. Today had already been preplanned with misery. There was no room for mine. I needed to snap out of it and carry on. Cate would need me, now more than before. I hit my palm against my forehead. "Why today? You're so stupid." The blows to my head did not take away the memories or the pain.

"Patti? Can I come in?" The squeak of the door startled me more than Cate.

"I'll be done in a minute." I sucked in the tears and let the water cascade over me, washing away the guilt and shame.

"I brought you some comfy clothes. I'll leave them on the

102

DEPENDING ON YOU

sink." I saw her shadow through the curtain. I know she wanted to talk, but I couldn't, not like this.

"Thanks." I turned off the water. "I'll be right out."

"Okay." She didn't move. "Is there anything I can do or get for you?"

"No, I'm fine." I pulled back the curtain and wrapped the towel around me and squeezed the water out of my hair. "How are you doing? Are you alright?" I stood in the tub, letting the water drip off me.

"I'm okay." Cate twirled her hair around her finger, the same thing she did when she was scared as a little girl.

"It's okay if you're not." I stepped onto the bathmat. "I'm sorry I got you into this mess."

"It's not your fault. I'm the one who did it. I'm the..." She covered her mouth. "Murderer."

"No, you're not. Don't say that." I held the towel tight against my body and pushed the images out of my mind. "I should have never made you come."

"Why did you call? What happened last night?" Cate wrapped her arms around her, looking for the warmth I couldn't get rid of.

"It's not important." I bent my head down and shook the water out of my hair.

"But I think it was. You sounded upset. And you looked..."

"I looked what? What are you trying to say?" I pulled my towel up, covering my chest.

"Like something happened to you." Cate looked down at her bare feet. "I want to help you."

"Nothing happened to me. I'd been drinking. That's all. I just needed a ride home and I didn't dare call my mom." I blew out my frustrations. "I'm fine, you're the one I'm worried about."

"Why won't you let me take care of you?" Cate hung her head. "You always take care of me, but I never get to take care of you. Why won't you let me?"

"Cate, nothing happened. There's nothing to help me with. I'm fine. Everything is fine." I bit the inside of my cheek and smiled. "We take care of each other. That's how it's always been." I reached for the clothes she brought me. "Like this, you let me borrow your clothes and take a shower."

"You're not borrowing anything, they're yours. You let me wear them home last week." Cate sighed. "I just don't want you to think I'm not here for you, because I am. I don't want to be the sad one with all the problems. I want to be equals."

"Cate, we are. You're my best friend. There's nothing that could ever change that. Now, if you don't mind, I'd like to get dressed."

"Alright." Cate closed the door behind her.

I saw myself in the mirror and hated every inch looking back at me. I put the sweatpants and T-shirt on and ran my fingers through my hair. I stepped over the dress that had fallen into a pile on the floor. I wrapped it up into a ball and covered it with my towel. "Hey, Cate, let's go start a fire in the barrel."

"Why? It's six in the morning." Cate got off the couch and eyed the pile in my hands. "What is that?"

"It's my dress. I want to burn it." I stood on my tippytoes and looked for a lighter on top of the refrigerator. "Come on, we can pretend we're camping."

"But why? Why are you burning your dress? Won't your mom be upset?"

"Cate, it's evidence. You should burn your clothes, too. Go

change and meet me outside." I pulled open the door and tossed the dress into the barrel, kicking the towel to the side. I scanned the yard to see if there were any nosey neighbors watching me. The coast was clear.

Cate tossed her pants and shirt on top of my dress. "Are you sure we should be doing this? Isn't it dangerous?"

"It's better than going to jail." I picked up the fire starter and sprayed it on the clothes. "Do you have any paper?"

Cate returned with a flyer from the local grocery store. "It's all I could find."

I lit the lighter and set the paper on fire. "Let's vow right here that we will never speak of what happened in that cemetery again."

"I promise, I won't tell anyone." Cate folded her arms.

"Blood sister's promise." I waited for Cate to nod before I tossed the paper into the barrel and took a step back as it ignited.

Cate stood next to me and leaned her head on my shoulder. "If you ever want to talk to me, you know I'm here, right?"

I put my arm around her waist. "Yes, Cate, I know." We watched the flames dance out of the barrel, taunting us, as if it wasn't done with us yet. The power in the flame was enough to destroy everything in its path. But not us. It was going to protect us and keep us safe.

Chapter Nineteen

CATE

We stood by the fire until it was out, watching as it held our secret. My secret. I hated that I got Patti mixed up in this mess. This was not how the best summer ever was supposed to start. "Are you ready to go inside?"

"Yeah, I guess it's safe to leave it now." Patti put her arm around me. "I love you."

"I'd understand if you didn't. I mean, I am a…"

"Would you shut up? The fire took it all away from us. Nothing happened last night. Nothing." She put her hand on my chin and turned my face. "Don't ever say that about yourself again."

I nodded, trying to fight back the tears. "Okay."

Dad opened the front door as we came in from the backyard. "Hey girls." He took his hat off and sat in his recliner. "What are you two doing up?"

Patti and I turned to look at each other. "Oh, we wanted to make the most of this beautiful day, Mr. Silver."

DEPENDING ON YOU

"Why are you home so late?" I sat on the couch in front of him. "Shouldn't you have been home hours ago?"

"What?" Dad rubbed his hand over his face. "I'm exhausted." He looked at Patti and opened his mouth. No sound came out.

I turned to Patti and saw her moving her eyes in my direction. "What is going on?"

"Oh, nothing, kiddo." Dad rocked his chair when he let out his breath.

"Your dad looks tired. We should go check on Sammy. I bet my mom is making pancakes again." She tugged on my arm.

"No, not yet. Tell me what that was about." I leaned forward and looked between Dad and Patti.

"What are you talking about, Cate? There's nothing going on." Patti stood up and held out her hand. "Let's give your dad a chance to rest and we can come back."

"No, it's fine, Patti. I don't think I should wait any longer." Dad rocked in his chair. "Cate, I don't know how to say this, so I'm just going to come out and say it."

Patti sat back down next to me and put her hand on my knee.

"Your mother." Dad closed his eyes and leaned forward in his chair. "Honey, your mom died."

"What? Mom? But I don't understand. I thought..." I heard what he said, but my heart and mind couldn't connect the dots.

"When she was found, she was already dead."

"How?" I fought back the urge to explode.

"We're waiting on the autopsy, but they're pretty sure it was an overdose." Dad covered his face with his weathered hands. "I'm so sorry, Catie Cat."

107

Patti rubbed my back and pulled me in for a hug. "I'm sorry."

"When did this happen? How do you already know?" I pushed back so I could see her face.

"Cate, I asked her not to tell you. I didn't want anything to ruin prom for you. Don't be mad at her. It's my fault. Be mad at me."

"Cate, I'm sorry. I wanted you to have the perfect night. You didn't need to worry about all of this any sooner. Time wasn't going to change anything."

"You were both in on this? How many other secrets are you keeping from me?" I squinted my eyes and glared at Dad, and then Patti. "What about the blood sister's promise? Does that mean nothing to you?"

"Cate, that's not fair. I was only trying to protect you." Patti folded her hands in her lap and looked away. A stray tear rolled down her face. "I'm sorry."

"This has nothing to do with Patti. If you want to be mad, be mad at me." Dad put his hands on his legs before standing up. "I shouldn't have told Patti. That was a mistake, but I don't regret not telling you."

"What about Sammy? Who's going to tell her?" I asked as Dad walked out the door.

"That's what I'm going to go do right now. Mrs. Thomas said she would help me." Dad shut the door before I could ask more questions.

"So, she knew, too? You both knew and you couldn't tell me?" I pulled away from Patti. "I thought you said there's no secrets between us?"

"It wasn't really a secret. It was just withholding information and not even for that long."

108

DEPENDING ON YOU

"Oh really? Withholding information? That's what we're calling it now." I stood up and folded my arms as I paced the living room. "First last night and now this? What else are you keeping from me?"

"Cate, it's not like that. I'm not keeping anything from you. Your dad showed up at my house right before you did. He didn't want to be sneaky, he only wanted you to be able to have a good time without having to worry about everything." Her voice cracked. "It's not like it was easy to know. It brought back all the memories of losing my dad. That's why I was in a funk last night. I couldn't stop thinking about my dad. Do you know what that does to a person?"

I sighed as I spun around on my heels. "I'm sorry, Patti. I don't want to fight. Everything is all screwed up. I don't even know what to do any more. I killed a man and now I'm punished by my mom dying." I rubbed my eyes. "But it's not me it's going to hurt, it's Sammy. Why can't I be the one who gets punished?"

"You're not being punished. She died before everything happened. I don't know why things happen the way they do. But what I do know is Sammy is going to need us." She placed her hand on my back. "I'm sorry."

I turned around and wrapped Patti in a hug. "I love you. I'm sorry. I shouldn't have been so upset with you." I nestled my head into her neck.

"We should go check on Sammy." She took my hand and brushed the tears off my face. "We'll get through this. I'm an old pro at this death thing." She chuckled. "I mean, I know what it feels like to lose someone you love."

"Except I didn't love her." I looked down at my feet and wiggled my toes. "I shouldn't say that."

109

"Why not? If it's true. She didn't act like a mother, so don't feel guilty for feeling relieved." Patti pushed the hair out of my face.

"I don't know what I think. I just want to make sure Sammy is okay. She loved Mom. They had a different relationship than we did."

"Well, that's probably because Sammy's still little. She was probably good to you when you were her age."

"Yeah, I guess." The more I thought about it, the more I couldn't remember any good memories with her. Now that she's gone, maybe Sammy has a chance at a normal life. It's too late for me.

Chapter Twenty

PATTI

"Did Cate tell you about the other night?" Jake wiggled his eyebrows.

"No, she didn't mention it." I tied my apron behind my back and put my hair into a ponytail.

"Really?" Jake's body deflated. "Oh."

"Don't get your panties in a bunch." I scrubbed chocolate syrup off the counter, avoiding eye contact. "She's had a lot going on."

"What do you mean? Is everything okay? Is that why she hasn't called me?" Jake put his hands in his pockets.

"Yeah, probably." I tossed the rag into the hamper and opened the window. "Looks like it's going to be a busy day."

When Jake put his hand on my shoulder, I turned around and hit him in the chest. "Whoa." He held his hands up. "Is everything alright?"

"Why wouldn't it be?"

"I don't know, maybe because you punched me. You're super jumpy." Jake crossed his arms. "You're acting different."

"What are you talking about? I'm not acting any way." I

111

JESSICA AIKEN-HALL

straightened my apron and put on my best fake smile to greet the customer standing in front of me.

Jake filled their order and shut the window. "Look, I know something is going on. I'm not opening this window until you tell me what's wrong."

I reached around him, trying to pry it back open. "Knock it off. We have to be available for the customers."

"There aren't any out there." He held the window down. "Come on, please tell me what's wrong."

I shook my head and fought back the tears. "No."

"Patti, come on. I know there's something. We're friends. You can trust me." He took a step closer to me.

"It's... it's just that I'm missing my dad. He didn't get to see me before prom, and he won't be at graduation tomorrow." I pushed the tears off my cheek and shrugged. "That's it."

"I'm sorry, Patti." Jake hung his head. "I know how bad that sucks. I've been missing my mom lately, too. Every time something good happens I can't wait to tell my mom, except I can't. And then it hurts all over again. My counselor told me it gets easier in time, but it hasn't."

"I've heard that, too. I hate when they say that. It's like they've never been in my head. They don't know. It's what they say when they don't know what else to say." I leaned on the counter and looked away. "Cate knows now, too."

"She knows what?" Jake joined me at the counter, being careful not to touch me.

"Her mom died. That's probably why she hasn't called you. She has a lot on her mind. And she's paying extra attention to her baby sister." I closed my eyes and rested my head on my hands. "I shouldn't have said anything. It's not up to me to tell you about this."

112

DEPENDING ON YOU

"Oh my god, that's awful. Right before graduation. She's got to be devastated." Jake crossed his arms and leaned his head against the cooler. "I need to talk to her."

"No, don't. Not yet. Wait until she tells you." I rubbed my eyes. "She doesn't want people feeling sorry for her. She'll be pissed at me for telling you."

"I don't understand. I thought we were dating. Isn't this something she should have told me?" Jake banged the back of his head on the door behind him.

"You're dating? Since when?"

"I don't know. I thought that's what happens when..." He ran his hand through his hair. "I really need to talk to her."

"You can't tell her I told you. Figure out a way to have her tell you." I put my hand on his arm. "Please don't let her know."

"I guess I'm confused why she doesn't want me to know. What's with the secrets?" Jake frowned. "I don't want to make it worse, but I want to help. Can't you just tell her you told me? You're best friends. Don't you think she'd understand?"

"There's so much more to it than that. I know she'll tell you when she's ready. If you care about her, you'll give her time."

"Fine." Jake folded his arms. "Will you at least tell me what I can do to help until she tells me?"

"Just be you. She cares about you. She told me she loves you."

"She said that? When?" Jake's smile returned.

"I need to keep my mouth shut." I pointed to the window. "Oh, look, we have customers."

"Are you trying to drive me crazy?" Jake opened the window and greeted the group of T-ball players.

I filled the orders as he handed me the slips. By the time the

113

line was gone, my hand was frozen. "Looks like I'm off the hook." I ran the hot water to thaw my fingers.

"I'll drop it." Jake held his hands up. "But remember, I'm here if either one of you need me."

"I know. You're a great guy. Cate's lucky to have you."

"Thanks." He smirked. "How are things with Andrew? He's looking forward to going out with you again."

"He's great, but I'm not looking to get in a relationship." I wiped the water off my hands. "It's not fair to either one of us to start something when I'm leaving at the end of the summer."

"You're going to give up on him that easy?" Jake asked.

"I'm not giving up on him. I'm not ready for anything serious. That's all. He's great. Now can we drop it?" I pushed the loose hair behind my ear.

"Okay, it's none of my business. I'll stop. Seems like I can't say anything right today." Jake looked at his watch. "Oh great, two more hours of this."

"I'm sorry I'm so snappy. I'm tired. It's been a lot the last few hours." I looked away before he saw the pain in my eyes. "I should have stayed home today."

"I can cover for you if you want. I know you must have a lot to do before tomorrow." He looked around the shop. "I'm sure I can handle it."

"No, that's not fair. If the rest of the T-ball teams show up, you'll be screwed. A couple more hours won't kill me." I dug my nails into my wrist as I forced a smile. I could manage two more hours.

Chapter Twenty-One
CATE

Every secret I ever had was written on my forehead. I was being swallowed alive by vulnerability and I couldn't keep my head above the shame. It felt like everyone knew. They knew what I did. They knew about my mom. The perfect bow I had tied around my life had let go. There was nothing left keeping the façade in place. I stood on the stage to accept my diploma and I wanted to fall into the deep, dark hole of despair and disappear.

"Miss Silver, you can go back to your seat now." Mr. Tillis smiled as he pointed me in the direction I should have been going.

All eyes were on me, picking my every move apart. Cheering and clapping surrounded me. My knees went weak, and my body hit the ground. Tammy Wilkerson bent down and hovered over me. "Are you ok?" She fanned me with her diploma.

"Yeah." I reached for her hand. "Will you help me up?"

Tammy walked with me until we reached our seats, depositing me carefully in my chair before going to hers.

Patti posed for pictures on the stage long enough to satisfy her mom and rushed to me. "What happened?"

"Overheated, I guess." I kicked off my shoes and ran my toes through the grass. "I'll be fine. Go sit down before you get in trouble."

"What are they going to do to me? Make me stay back?" She raised her brow.

"Don't cause a scene." I surveyed the area. No one seemed to care she was breaking the rules. "Go on."

After the last name was called, the class of 1998 tossed our caps and cheered. Groups of kids rushed together, but I couldn't move. Patti came up behind me and put her arm around me. "Let's go find our people."

"What people?" I closed my eyes to try to channel enough calmness to get through the morning.

"My mom, your dad, Sammy. You know, those people." She linked her arm with mine. "And Jake."

"I don't want to see him." I put my head down and walked with Patti through the sea of people.

"Why not? I thought you loved him." Patti jabbed me in the side and laughed. "He really likes you."

"Yeah, whatever." I kept my eyes down, trying my best to avoid everyone.

"Cate, come on. I know you're sad and stuff, but sometimes it's good to get your mind off things."

"I don't want to. I can't." The feet in front of mine looked familiar. When I glanced up, I saw Sammy on Dad's shoulders.

"Congratulations, girls." Mrs. Thomas handed us each a bouquet of pink roses.

"Thank you." A tear drop soaked into the white tissue

DEPENDING ON YOU

paper. I stuck my nose in to smell the sweet fragrance and hide my emotions.

"Yeah, congratulations. I'm proud of both of you girls." Dad hung on to Sammy's ankles as she bounced on his back.

"Proud Sissy." Sammy squealed. "Good job."

"Thanks Sammy." Patti reached up and tickled her.

"How about we go back to our house and have some lunch?" Mrs. Thomas put her arm around Patti.

"I don't feel very good. I think I want to go home." I flashed Dad a smile. "But you guys can go."

"Come on, please?" Patti pulled at my hand. "I want to celebrate with you. At least for a little while?"

"Okay." I hung my head and submitted.

Sammy, Patti, and I squished together in the back of Dad's Ford Taurus. The same car I drove a few nights ago. The night that everything changed. Mrs. Thomas and Dad got in the front to make the short drive.

In the distance, I heard someone yell my name. I closed my eyes so I wouldn't see who I was ignoring. "Cate, it looks like someone is looking for you." Dad looked at me through the rearview mirror.

I looked out my window and saw Jake flagging down the car. "Let's go, we don't need to wait around here."

"Cate, at least tell the poor boy hello." Dad turned off the car. "Don't be rude."

"I'm not in the mood." I gritted my teeth and waved at Jake. "Can we please get out of here?"

Jake jogged the rest of the way to the car, holding onto the top of his cap. "Hey Mr. Silver." He stopped to catch his breath. "I'm Jake." He extended his hand. "It's nice to meet you."

117

"Nice to meet you, too." Dad raised his brow and smiled at me in the rearview mirror. "We were just about to go have a..."

I rolled down my window. "Hi Jake. We were just leaving, but how about I give you a call later?"

Jake bent down to look into my window. "Okay, I'd like that." His gleaming, white teeth flashed in my face. "Have a great day, you guys." He tapped his hand on the window and walked away.

"He seems nice." Mrs. Thomas turned to smile. "Are you sure you don't want to invite him for lunch?"

"No, I'm not up to entertaining anyone." I rolled my window up and watched Jake fade into the crowd.

"Okay, sweetie, but if you change your mind, he's more than welcome." She turned her attention to Patti. "Do you want to see if Andrew would like to join us?"

"No, Mom. I think this car full is enough." Patti tucked her hair behind her ear. "What do you say Sammy, do you want to start the party off with some ice cream?"

Sammy rocked in her car seat. "Ice cream! Ice cream!"

I covered my ears. "Nice going, now we're going to have to have dessert and then more dessert."

"That sounds pretty good." Patti tickled Sammy. "Sorry, Mom, we won't be needing lunch. We only have room for ice cream."

"You girls are silly. Don't you know that's not how it works? You can't have two desserts when there's time for three." She put her sunglasses on and turned to Dad. "Do you think we could stop at the store? It looks like there's been a change of plans."

"You don't have to do that. I'm sure whatever you have

DEPENDING ON YOU

planned will be great." Dad looked back at us. "Isn't that right, girls?"

"Yeah, we're fine." I answered for all of us.

Mrs. Thomas put her hand on Dad's arm. "Really, it's no trouble. I think three desserts sounds like a marvelous idea."

Dad and Mrs. Thomas left us in the car and went to fulfil Sammy's request. "You're a spoiled little..."

"Cate." Patti hit my leg. "Don't be like that."

"I want her to be my mommy." Sammy rocked in her seat. "Mommy and Daddy. Mommy and Daddy."

"That would be nice, wouldn't it? Then we could all be real sisters." Patti took Sammy's hand. "I'd be happy to share my mom with you anytime you want."

Sammy put her head on Patti. "I love you."

"I love you, too." Patti kissed her head. "You're the best little sister ever."

I pressed myself against the window and tried to disappear. It was too much effort to even hold my head up. I needed to find a place to hide, where I didn't have to talk to anyone or pretend. Carrying this secret took everything I had. I wasn't sure how much longer before it seeped out somewhere. My only wish was to make sure I'm the only one who will take the fall. I couldn't live with myself if I destroyed another person's life. Especially one I loved.

119

Chapter Twenty-Two

CATE

The first month of summer sailed past me while I stayed curled up in my bed. The only time I left my room was to take care of Sammy, but it'd been weeks since I left the house. I asked Patti to tell Jake I couldn't see him anymore, but she wouldn't. She said it would make it too awkward working with him.

Laying on the floor, I counted the ceiling tiles in the kitchen while Sammy sung her ABC's. It was the only place to stay cool in the mid July heat. A knock on the front door made me freeze. Dad wouldn't be home for another six hours. "Sammy, shh." I held my finger to my lips.

She shook her head and ran to the door. Her tiny hand twisted the handle, opening the door in slow motion. I was too slow. "Hi, Sammy." Mrs. Thomas bent down to Sammy's level. She pushed her way into the house. "Cate, it's so good to see you." She scooped me into a hug.

"Hi Mrs. Thomas. Sorry I haven't..."

"Oh honey, don't apologize." She took my hands and gave

them a little shake. "I can't imagine what you've been going through. Well, I can, but I know it's different for everyone."

"I'm fine." I pushed up a fake smile.

"You don't have to lie to me. I want to be here for you. I'm only a short walk away. You and Sammy are welcome over to the house anytime. You don't have to go through this alone." She licked her thumb and rubbed it on my face.

"Thank you, Mrs. Thomas." I turned my head and cleared my throat. "We're fine, really. There's no need to worry about us."

"Okay. But the offer is there, for both of you. Any time, day, or night. You can just keep me company. I won't even ask you any pesky questions." Mrs. Thomas took Sammy's hand. "How about we go get some ice cream?"

"Yeah!" Sammy jumped in place. "Ice cream!"

"What do you say Cate, do you want to join us? I know Patti would love to see you." She scooped Sammy up into her arms.

"No, I think I'll stay home. There's so much to do around here." I picked up a dirty paper towel and rubbed it on the counter.

"It can wait. I'll come back here after and help. Patti will be leaving in a couple weeks. I know you're sad, but sometimes being with a good friend is all you need. I'm not going to take no for an answer. Go get ready. Sammy and I will be outside playing." Mrs. Thomas took Sammy's hand.

I rubbed my forehead to push away the headache. It wasn't that I didn't want to see Patti, it was more that I knew I wasn't good for her. In my room I found the cleanest pair of pants off my floor and put them on. My T-shirt was clean enough, so I ran a brush through my tangled hair. "You're such a mess." I

121

flipped off the light and found Mrs. Thomas and Sammy in the back yard.

"It's such a beautiful day. What do you say we walk?" She held out her hand and Sammy attached to it like Velcro.

"Sure." Sammy latched on to me with her other hand.

"How's your dad been doing?" Mrs. Thomas asked.

"I don't know. We haven't seen much of him. He's been busy at work I guess." I squinted my eyes to keep the glare of the sun out.

"Oh, that's right. I bet he's been working on that murder case." She twisted her lips and shook her head. "Such a shame. And I thought this was a safe town."

I attempted to gather my composure. "He doesn't talk about work."

"That makes sense. He's been doing it long enough to know he shouldn't bring that stuff home with him."

"Yeah, I guess so." I kicked at the pebbles on the sidewalk.

"Be careful. I mean, no one knows what happened. The killer could be anywhere. Keep your eyes open. That's what I tell Patti." Mrs. Thomas swung Sammy's hand in hers. "You can never be too careful."

"Right." I tucked my hair behind my ear. "It could have been an accident."

"It could have. You're right. We will have to wait and see. I know the police are hard at work keeping us safe."

Sammy broke free from our hands and ran the rest of the way to the ice cream shop.

Patti raced out the door and held her arms out. "Sammy! I've missed you."

Sammy's laughter followed behind her like a cloud of dust. "Patti!"

122

DEPENDING ON YOU

Patti stood up with Sammy in her arms and did a spin before setting her down. "Wow, you've gotten so big."

"I have not." Sammy put her hands on her hips and scowled. "I'm little."

"You're right." Patti laughed. "Hey, Cate." Her smile made my heart ache.

"Hi." I looked away to ward off the looming agony.

"What are you doing? I get out of work soon. Do you want to hang out?" Patti asked the question I had longed to hear so many weeks ago. The one I needed but didn't deserve.

"I've got a lot to do back at the house." I stared down at my sneakers. The ones I bought with her two summers ago at the mall.

"How about after we have some ice cream, I take Sammy back home and help out? I don't have anything planned for the rest of the day. I'd love to help and that way you'd have time to spend some time with each other." Mrs. Thomas waved at the person in the window.

I squinted to see who it was. The pit of my stomach dropped to my knees. Jake stuck his head out the window and motioned for us to come over. I took a deep breath and closed my eyes. He was the last person I had expected to see. Mrs. Thomas put her arm around my waist and ushered me to the window.

"Hi Cate." Jake's smile beamed. "It's so nice to see you. I tried calling you a few times." He ran his hand through his hair. "Did you get the messages I left?"

"Sorry, I've been busy." My phony smile faded as fast as I plastered it on my face.

"Well, now that you're here, what do you say we make plans? I have tomorrow off. We could go to the river and have a

123

JESSICA AIKEN-HALL

picnic or something. Whatever you want." The eagerness was too hard to pass up.

"Sure." I looked to Mrs. Thomas. "Would you be able to watch Sammy?"

"Of course. Anytime you need." Her cheeks lifted.

"Great." Jake pulled himself back through the window. "What can I get you lovely ladies?"

"Chocolate." Sammy demanded. "Extra chocolate."

Patti went back inside. "I'll get it. I know just what she likes."

After Sammy got her special bowl of ice cream, Patti came outside to join us while Jake filled the rest of our orders. "So, that will be fun." She sat on the bench next to me.

"Hey, I'm sorry..."

She put her hand on my arm. "Don't be. I get it. I've been a little messed up, too. No hard feelings. Sisters forever."

"And ever?" I wiped the corner of my eye.

"And ever." Patti put her arm around me and pulled me close. "We're in this together. No matter what."

Chapter Twenty-Three

PATTI

The last few weeks without Cate made me miss her even more. The fact that she was so quick to push me away stung. "There were so many days I wanted to come over." I hung my head. "But I didn't want to bother you."

"You could never bother me." Cate closed her eyes before looking away from me. "I didn't want to ruin anything else for you."

"What are you talking about? You didn't ruin anything for me. Nothing happened, remember?"

She sighed. "I wish it were that easy. Nothing I do makes that night go away. I don't even know who I am anymore. Today's the first day I left my house since graduation."

"Really? You've been home all that time? What have you been doing?"

"Taking care of Sammy." She shrugged. "Sleeping. That's about it."

"I don't understand. Why don't you want to be with me?" I forced a smile to fight back the waterworks brewing inside.

125

"Patti, it's not you, it's me. I'm bad. I'm... I'm..." Cate covered her eyes.

"You're hurting. You're scared. You're not damaged. You're still you." I pushed the hair out of her face. "Please don't desert me. I need you. I leave in fifteen days. I can't stand that we lost so much time together. And for what?"

"I'm sorry." She wrapped her arms around my neck. "I didn't know what to do. I felt so alone."

"Me, too. I figured you hated me or something." I blew out the breath I had been holding the last few weeks. "From this day forward, we don't do that ever again. Don't assume we're upset with each other. I have your back and you have mine."

"I always have." She sniffled. "That's what kept me away. I was trying to protect you."

"Cate..."

"Yeah?"

I held my hand up and paused. "It's nothing. I love you so much."

"Same." Her smile brought out the sparkle in her eyes.

"So, you haven't talked to Jake either?" I already knew the answer. He hadn't stopped talking about her. Every day it was the same conversation.

"Nobody. Just Sammy and my dad." She chuckled. "If I have to hear about Barney one more time." She punched her hand. "I'm going to lose my mind."

"Oh man, that sounds horrible."

"Yeah, let's just say we're not one big happy family." She snorted. "God, I've missed you."

"So have I. You know who I've got to talk to? Jake." I rolled my eyes. "If I have to hear him cry about you, I'll lose my mind. I'd rather hear a purple dinosaur sing."

DEPENDING ON YOU

"He talks about me? A lot?" Cate sat on the edge of the couch. "What does he say?"

"What doesn't he say is the better question. He didn't know what he did to upset you. I reminded him that you had a lot on your mind, and he calmed down for a while, but he misses you. I'm glad you're going to hang out tomorrow."

Cate picked at the loose thread on the cushion. "I'm going to tell him I don't want to see him again."

"Why Cate? Why would you do that? He really likes you. It will break his heart. And I know you like him. I can see it when you mention his name."

"I don't want to live a lie with him, and I'll never be able to tell him the truth." She held her face in her hands. "I'll never be able to be with anyone."

I rubbed her back. "Oh Cate. That's not true. You'll find your special someone. And it might be Jake. It's not lying, it's only withholding information."

"It's more than that. I killed a man. That will always be a part of who I am. There's no getting around it. You're the only one who will ever know." She pushed a breath through her pursed lips.

"He doesn't have to know. No one does."

"The murder is still under investigation. And my dad is the one in charge of the case."

"He is?" I asked.

"Apparently." She lifted her shoulders. "I didn't know that was the case he had been working on, but your mom told me. If she knows about the case, sooner or later everyone is going to. It's just a matter of time before they figure out it was me."

"There is nothing there linking you to the crime. There's no

127

way they will pin it on you." I tapped my lips as I thought. "What if you get your dad to close the case somehow?"

"How? He doesn't talk about work with me."

"If he's talking to my mom about it, maybe it's something I can get her to talk to him about." I leaned back against the cushions and thought through the different scenarios. "We could get your dad and my mom together. If he's busy with her, maybe he wouldn't want to put so much energy into the case."

Cate curled up her nose. "Gross. No. I don't want to do that. Besides, my mom just died. He's not going to want to date anyone this soon."

I raised my brow. "Really? You think so? I'm pretty sure they like each other. She spends a lot of her time talking about your dad."

"I don't even know what to think about that. I love your mom, but that's weird. Your mom belongs here, and my dad belongs at my house. They shouldn't mix environments."

"This isn't science class. It's chemistry." I wiggled my eyebrows.

"That's the same thing." Cate rolled her eyes.

"It is not. I took two separate classes. They're definitely different."

She tossed a throw pillow at me. "Whatever. It doesn't matter. But no. That's a horrible plan."

"Come on, it's the perfect plan. My mom could use the company while I'm gone."

"Then I'll come stay here with her. My dad will not."

"He's a grown man. If they like each other, I don't think there's anything we can do to stop it." I rubbed my eyes. "It might be the only way to keep him occupied enough to ditch the whole case."

DEPENDING ON YOU

"I'm pretty certain it doesn't work that way. And I don't want to think about the two of them rolling around naked together."

"My eyes, my eyes." I covered my face and laughed.

"See, that's what I'm talking about. It's not what I want to think about."

"Okay, that's fair. But if they do it on their own," I shrugged, "there's nothing we can do about it."

"We can deal with that if the time comes. But I don't want to make any love connections happen to save myself. I'd rather go to jail than hear their sweet love making." Cate stuck out her tongue and gagged. "Enough about this. How have you been?"

"The same. You know." I pulled my legs under me. "Mostly getting ready for college. Mom's taken me shopping every weekend. I have no idea how I'm going to get it all down there, or where I'll fit it."

"Have you heard who you're sharing your dorm with?" Cate eased into her old self, like nothing had happened. This was the Cate that I missed.

"Yeah, Amy someone. She's from Wisconsin. We've talked on the phone a couple times."

"You have? I didn't know they did that." Cate twirled her hair around her index finger.

"They don't, not really. But Mom pulled some strings. She knows someone who knows someone and got Amy's number."

"That must be a relief. Right?"

"I guess so. It's not like I know her, though. We only talked on the phone a couple of times. And she seems... dorky." I laughed. "I know that's mean."

"It's not mean. Not everyone can be as cool as us." Cate

129

smiled. "Dorky is probably a good quality. That way she won't get you into any trouble."

"No, I don't need her for that. Trouble has a way of finding me all on its own."

"What happened that night?" Cate's smile faded. "What made you so afraid?"

I wrinkled my nose. "Nothing. I already told you that. I had a few too many drinks and I didn't want my mom to know."

"Are you sure? Because I'm here if you need to tell me something. Did Andrew do something to you?" Cate picked at her fingernails and waited for my answer.

"Cate, I'm sure. I wish I never called you that night. I know what happened was my fault."

"No, it's not. How was it your fault? I'm the one who ran him over. I should have been watching where I was going. I should have been paying attention."

"But if I hadn't gotten myself in that situation, I never would have needed to call you, and you wouldn't have hit anyone. See, it's my fault. Just as much as it is yours. Maybe even more."

"You're not going to take the blame like that. So what if you had a few drinks? You needed me, and I screwed everything up. It's my mess and I don't want you to take responsibility for any of it. Do you promise me that you won't?"

"We're in this together. We can't change what happened. How about neither one of us take the fall for it?" I stretched my arms over my head and yawned. "Why don't we go get a pizza? I'm starving." I stood up and pulled Cate off the couch and out of the pile of destruction she was working so hard to have land on her. I'd find a way to protect her. I had to.

130

Chapter Twenty-Four

CATE

The sky was littered with storm clouds. The sunshine we had hoped for would have to push through the darkness, like a lotus through the mud. I tossed a stone into the river and watched the ripples as I waited for Jake to arrive. The rain droplets landed on the top of my head as a cloud passed over me. I leaned my face to the sky, hoping the water would wash away my sins with it.

"Hi beautiful." Jake came down the path with his hand behind his back.

I got to my feet and walked the rest of the way to him. "Hi."

He handed me a bouquet of flowers. "I picked these before I came."

The bunch of wildflowers were wrapped with a paper towel around the stems. "They're beautiful."

"I wanted to buy you flowers, but that's too easy. I climbed through a field full of snakes to get those for you. A symbol of my love for you. I'm willing to work for it."

I blinked the tears out of my eyes, thankful for the rain. "That's sweet."

"Can I give you a hug?" Jake held his arms out.

I stepped into his embrace. The feel of his arms around me brought me back to the dance floor. I nestled my head into his neck and inhaled the scent of his skin. I melted deeper into his arms and sobbed.

He tightened his arms before softening his hold on me. He rubbed my back. "I need to tell you something."

I sniffled into his shoulder. "I do, too."

"I know about your mom, and I'm so sorry. I know what it's like." He took a step back and took my hands in his. "I lost my mom, too. I didn't want to tell you before, because I didn't want you to feel sorry for me."

"Are you saying you feel sorry for me?"

"No. Well, yes, but not in a bad way. I feel sad for you because I know how bad it hurts to lose someone you love. I feel sad that I didn't tell you about my mom before now. And I feel sad that you have had to go through this alone." He yanked on my arms. "And I love you. I know it might be too soon, but I need you to know. I know how important it is to say the things you need to say before it's too late."

I felt my heart rip out of my chest when I looked into his eyes. I dropped my head and bit my bottom lip. Sobs took place of my words. My body trembled as the emotion spilled out. I couldn't say what he needed to hear. I couldn't tell him what I needed to say.

"I don't want you to say it if you don't. I just wanted you to know I do. If you're not ready for anything serious I understand. But please don't shut me out. I want to be there for you. I know how much it hurts and I can help. I can be your tour guide through the pain." He pushed the tears off my cheek.

DEPENDING ON YOU

"Please at least let me help you. Not out of sympathy, but out of love and respect. At least think about it."

I nodded. "Okay."

"I'll wait for you, Cate. For as long as you need."

"No, I don't want you to do that." I scrunched up my face. "Don't let me waste your time."

"You're not wasting my time. If you don't want to date, at least be my friend. I can keep Patti's place warm while she's away." His dimples were too hard to resist. "Give me a chance."

"Okay." I took his hand. "We can be friends but I'm not ready to do what we did the other night again."

"I understand." Jake put his arm around my waste. "Do you want to go swimming?"

"In the rain?" I raised my brow.

"We're already wet." He shrugged. "Besides, there's something magical about swimming in the rain. It's like you don't know where the water starts or ends. It's one big circle." He squeezed his arm around me and broke out in a melody. "It's the circle of life."

"Oh my goodness." I shook my head.

"What can I say? My little sister loves that movie. It kind of grows on you after the hundredth time you've seen it." He laughed.

"Yeah, I get it. I dream about Barney and his friends."

"Should I be jealous?" Jake put his hand on his hip.

"No, you don't have anything to worry about." I laughed. "Did you bring something to change into?"

"I'll wear what I have on, it's already wet." He kicked off his sneakers. "What are you going to wear?"

"I came prepared. My bathing suit is on under this." I pulled off my t-shirt and slid off my jeans.

133

"Is it okay if I swim in my boxers?" He pulled off his shirt. "I promise I won't try anything."

"It's fine." I bit the inside of my cheek to try and pull my attention away from his body. The same one that I felt so comfortable with just weeks earlier. Before everything changed.

Jake raced into the water and went under. He shook his hair out of his eyes when he came back up. "Get in. The water's great."

I tiptoed in, with my arms wrapped around my waste. "It's freezing." My teeth chattered.

"Oh, it's not that bad." Jake splashed water at me.

"Hey, knock it off." I held my hands up to block his attempts.

He gasped. "God, you're gorgeous." He looked away. "Sorry. I didn't mean to say that."

I couldn't keep the smile off my face. I splashed him before I went under. "Oops, sorry." I swam to him, keeping my head above water.

"I guess I deserved that." He crouched to keep himself submerged. "I don't know why I never come here."

"Because it's Patti's and my spot. No one else is allowed." I treaded water to stay near him. "We've spent so much time here. We've been coming here since we were old enough to leave the house alone."

"You two are something else. I bet you have so many memories."

"We do." I floated in the water and watched the sun poke out through the clouds. "More than a lifetime worth, already."

"There's always room for more." Jake held his arms out and looked up. "The rain stopped."

DEPENDING ON YOU

"I guess it did. So much for your circle of water crap." I kicked my feet by him, splashing him in the face.

He went under water and appeared next to my head and spit water next to me. "Thank you for sharing your special place with me."

"Thank you for being so understanding about everything." I rolled into an upright position and put my arms around his waist. "I'm glad you're not mad at me. I never wanted to hurt you."

"You could never hurt me." He kissed the top of my head. "I didn't take it personally."

"I'm glad. I don't deserve you." I had to keep reminding myself that. I didn't want to start something I couldn't finish. Things were too good. The only way to fix it was to break it.

Chapter Twenty-Five
PATTI

The last of my things were loaded into Mom's car. All that was left was an eight-hour drive, then my new life would begin. I wiped the sweat off my brow and looked over at Cate. "I'm going to miss you so much."

"Me, too." Cate folded her hands in front of her and looked away. "You're going to have so much fun, though. It's going to be good."

"Are you sure you don't want to come with us? We could rearrange some stuff." Mom started moving boxes around.

"No, I really shouldn't, not this time. Dad needs me to watch Sammy." Cate smiled. "I'll plan a time real soon."

"You better." I blinked to keep the tears from falling. "The sooner the better." I went over to Cate and pulled her into my arms. "If you need anything, remember Mom's still here. You can use my room anytime."

"Okay. Thank you." She gave me a squeeze before taking a step back. "It's not goodbye, it's see you later."

"That's right." I pulled out a slip of paper and handed it to her. "This is my number, call me. If you don't, I'll call you."

DEPENDING ON YOU

Cate rubbed her eyes and nodded. "I will."

"Okay, Patti, we've got to get on the road." Mom stood between us and brought us together for a group hug. "These four years are going to fly by. Before you know it, you'll be back together."

I kissed Cate's cheek and rushed away. "I love you."

"I love you, too." Cate waved as Mom and I pulled out of the driveway. I turned around in my seat and watched her fade into the distance.

"It will get easier." Mom put her hand on my leg. "This is only a small hiccup in your life. So many adventures await you."

"I never imagined we wouldn't go to the small college. We always planned on sharing our dorm." I sank into my seat. "Everything is so different than what I thought it'd be."

"Oh, honey, life has a funny way of changing everything around on us. Just when you think you know what's going to happen, something else comes along."

I stared out the window and watched as everything I knew slipped away. The streets Cate and I walked on. The river we swam in so many summers. And the cemetery that changed everything. I gasped for air when the thoughts swallowed me alive.

"Patti, it's going to be okay. I know it's hard. You've accomplished so much and with so many obstacles. I'm so proud of you." She turned on the radio. "How about some music? That always makes things better." She turned up the volume and hit the button to scan the stations.

"Leave it here." I pressed the button to listen to Tom Petty's *You Don't Know How it Feels*.

"Good find." Mom bobbed her head to the beat. "You know, your father loved Tom Petty and the Heartbreakers."

137

JESSICA AIKEN-HALL

"I know." My sadness eased as the lyrics soothed my soul.

When the song finished the top of the hour news took over the airwaves. Mom reached over and turned the volume up. "Breaking news in the Lawrenceville murder case." My heart sank as the headline blasted between my ears.

Mom's back stiffened as she sat up to listen.

I fidgeted in my seat, waiting for the announcer to speak. "Details in the case up next."

"Good Lord, why do they do those things to me?" Mom's posture softened. "I just want to know what happened to that poor man, and if there's any threat to the rest of us."

"Yeah." Panic radiated through me as I awaited the news.

"After a thorough investigation, the murder at the Heaven Hill Cemetery has been ruled a homicide. Police are asking members of the community to report any suspicious activity in the area on the night of June fifth. This appears to be an isolated incident. There is no threat to the community."

"Are you kidding me? That's all they have to say? Not to worry?" Mom scoffed.

"If they say not to worry, don't worry. I'm sure Mr. Silver would let you know if there was something you needed to be concerned about. I mean he wouldn't say that if it weren't true. Cate and Sammy live in town. I know he'd make sure they're safe."

"You're right." Mom nodded. "It's hard to believe, that's all. For the past few weeks I've been on edge wondering who could have done it, or if I'm standing next to them at the grocery store. It's unnerving, but if Norm says it's nothing to worry about, then I should trust him."

"Norm?" I raised my brow. "You call him Norm?"

138

DEPENDING ON YOU

"What am I supposed to call him? That's his name, silly." The smile spread across Mom's face.

"You like him, don't you?" I turned the radio down. "It's okay with me if you do."

"Of course, I like him. We've known each other for years. We're practically family."

"That's not what I mean. Don't you want to make more of your friendship? Keep each other company? Tell him about your day?"

Mom laughed. "Oh, dear girl, no. I mean Norm's a great friend, and I love him, but it will never be more than that."

"Are you sure it's not worth a shot?" I lifted my shoulders. "Cate and Sammy could use a mom and you both could stand some company."

"Honey, Norm just lost his wife. I'm sure he's not ready to date, and if he were, I'm not interested in him. Not like that." Mom smiled. "We can all be a family without it getting weird."

"Mom, it's not weird. Mr. Silver is a nice guy, and Cate and Sammy love you." I leaned my head back. "It could fix so many things."

"Nothing needs fixing. I love Cate and Sammy. I'll be there for them whenever they need me. I'll listen to Norm anytime he wants to talk, but I am not romantically interested in him."

"It was worth a shot." I dropped my shoulders with a sigh.

"I'll be fine, you know. Sure, I'll be lonely without you, but you don't need to worry about me. You don't need to fix everything for everyone. It's not your job." She reached over and put her hand on my knee.

"I don't do that." I crossed my arms. "I'm not a fixer, I'm a screwup."

139

"Patti, don't say that. That's not true. You've always been the one to help others. You're a mother hen."

"I'm an only child. How can I be a mother hen? I don't have anyone to mother."

"Cate, Sammy, me." Mom smiled. "It's not a bad thing. It means you have a good heart. But it's time you take care of you. Things were hard after your dad died, and I'm sorry I fell apart for so long. That wasn't fair to you."

"Mom, don't be sorry. It was hard when Dad died. You did the best you could."

"See, you're trying to take care of me. I know I let you down, but I hope you know how much I love you. God blessed me when I had you." Mom patted my knee. "I knew you were going to be special the minute I set eyes on you."

"I'm the way I am because of you and Dad. I got lucky having you guys for parents. I couldn't have wished for a better family. I guess that's why I wanted to share you with Cate and Sammy."

"And you do. I think of those girls as my own. The world is a better place because you're in it." Mom brushed the tears out of her eye. "Don't let anyone ever change you."

Mom's advice had come a few weeks too late. I was already changed with no hope of returning to normal. I desperately wanted to be who she thought I was. She was the last person I wanted to disappoint.

Summer
of
2018

Chapter Twenty-Six
CATE

"Oh, for Christ's sake." Dad pointed the remote at the TV and increased the volume. "Why the hell do people have to dig up the past?"

Patti and I looked at each other as the press conference interrupted our reminiscing. My tongue swelled in the back of my mouth as I tried to catch my breath. Patti took my hand and gave it a squeeze.

Dad sighed. "Can you believe this crap? No one gave a damn about any of this for the past twenty years, and now that I can't go down to the police station to smarten them up, this happens." He tossed the remote on the bed. "Unbelievable."

"Why are they doing it? Wasn't the case solved?" Patti asked.

"No, it's a cold case. But there's no reason to open it. A waste of taxpayer's money." Dad shook his head. "This town has gone to hell. There's no way I would have allowed this to happen if I were still in charge down there."

"Do you remember much about the case?" Patti sat on the edge of the couch.

142

DEPENDING ON YOU

"Every detail." Dad rested his head on the pillow. "There was nothing. That kid is chasing ghosts."

"Nothing?" Patti looked at me and nodded. "So, they're not going to find anything."

"Not a thing. There wasn't any evidence collected at the scene, and the body has been buried for twenty years."

"If they exhumed the body, would they find anything?" I pulled my shirt away from my neck.

"I don't know." Dad sighed. "There's no good reason to do that. But when money is involved, there's no telling what they'll do."

"Can't someone stop them?" Patti asked what I was thinking.

"No, if it's what the kid wants, and he's got the cash, they'll do whatever he asks." Dad reached for the remote. "But I guess it doesn't even matter."

I went over to his bed and handed him the remote. "It does matter. I know how hard you worked on this case."

He turned off the TV. "I did. I spent months on it, and I put it to rest when there was nothing left to do."

"Is there anyone left down there that worked on the case with you?" Patti came over to the bed and crossed her arms.

"No, everything has changed." Dad closed his eyes. "If they find something after all these years, I won't be able to live it down." He laughed. "Guess that doesn't even matter anymore."

"It matters, Dad." I sat on his bed and picked at the blankets. "I know you did your best."

"What can we do to help?" Patti rubbed the top of his hand. "Is there someone we could talk to for you?"

"The only person who can stop this is that kid." Dad

143

JESSICA AIKEN-HALL

shrugged. "But from my experience little brats don't stop until they have what they want."

"The kid?" Patti sucked in air through her nose. "Okay."

"What are you thinking?" I asked Patti.

"I've got to find him and have a talk with him." She paced the living room. "It's the only thing we can do."

"Why would you do that?" Dad squinted. "It won't matter once I'm dead. These things don't happen fast."

"Don't talk like that, Dad." I rubbed my forehead.

"You deserve to keep your legacy intact. You were the best detective in this town. We can't let some kid take that from you." Patti looked at her watch. "Cate, can I have your keys?"

"Why? What are you going to do?" I got up and looked out the window. "I can't leave until Sammy gets back."

"Don't be crazy, Cate. I'm fine. You don't need to babysit me." Dad tried to sit up.

"See, this is why you can't be alone. What if you need something? Or the house burns down, or someone breaks in?" I threw my hands up. "Where did Sammy go?"

"I don't know." Dad reached for the remote on his bed. "I'm fine. Really."

I adjusted the head of his bed and moved the control where he could reach it. "I don't want you here alone. I wouldn't be able to live with myself if something happened to you."

"I can go by myself." Patti put her hand on my back. "You don't need to leave him. I can handle this."

"No," I snapped. "You don't need do this. I can."

"I want to help," Patti said.

"Then stay here with Dad while I go find the kid." I grabbed my keys off the counter. "Let me do this."

"There's nothing to say, remember?" Patti raised her brow.

DEPENDING ON YOU

"Yeah, I remember. I won't do anything crazy. I just want to meet him and see what he's really after." I gave Dad a kiss on the forehead. "I'll take care of this."

"Catie Cat, you don't have to do this." Dad reached his hand out. "Come back. There are more important things to do with your time."

"No, there's really not. This is something I need to do." I closed the door behind me and blew out a rush of anxiety into the fresh air.

Patti followed behind me. "Cate, are you sure you're up for this?"

"I don't have much choice." The keys dangled in my hand.

"You're not going to..." Patti crossed her arms. "You know, tell him?"

"Not yet. But I need to meet him and see if there's anything I can do to help." I opened the car door. "It's the least I can do."

"I don't think you should go. At least not yet. Wait until Sammy comes home, and I'll go with you."

"No, there's no time to wait. He might still be at the police station. I need to do this. It might be the only way I can stay out of trouble until I lose Dad."

Patti dropped her shoulders. "Okay. I trust you."

"Good, because if you don't, I'm screwed." I got in the car and backed out of the driveway. Patti waved before going back into the house. I turned the stereo on and cranked the volume. I sang along with Joan Osborne to *One of Us* as I tried to ease my nerves. I didn't know what I was going to say, or how I was going to convince this kid to talk to me. This was when having Sammy with me might have come in handy. She was the perfect carrot to dangle in front of any young guy's nose.

I pulled my car into the parking lot at the police station. For

145

a second it was like being a kid waiting for Dad to come out and give me money for dinner. I gripped the steering wheel and emptied my lungs. "You can do this." I put the keys in my purse and pushed my hair around to make myself presentable.

My body trembled as I stood by my car. It wasn't too late to leave and take Patti up on her offer. I didn't have to do this alone. I closed my eyes and my body flooded with panic. I couldn't keep living like this. The time to own up to my past was here. If I was ready or not. "Just do it."

"Excuse me, ma'am, are you alright?" The quiet voice came from behind me.

When I turned around, I saw him. My heart sank. There was no turning back now. I turned around and extended my hand. "Hi, I'm Cate Silver."

He slid his hand into mine and gave it a quick shake. "Silver?" He raised his brow. "Any relation to Detective Silver?"

"He's my dad. And you are?" I tilted my head as I waited to hear what I already knew.

"Silas Hart." He put his hands in his pockets. "Your dad doesn't work here still, right?"

"No, he's retired." I held my purse strap tight. "Why do you ask?"

"Well, I don't know if you've seen the news or not, but I'm looking to solve my father's murder and I was told your dad was the lead detective on the case."

"Yeah, I've heard." I worked up a smile. "I was here to see you, actually."

"You're here to see me? Why?" Silas pulled his phone out of his pocket and pushed a button.

"What are you doing? I don't want to be recorded." I held up my hand.

146

DEPENDING ON YOU

"I was checking the time." He showed me the face of his phone. "I'm supposed to meet with the PI my parents hired for me in twenty minutes. Will this take longer than that?"

"PI?" I scrunched up my face.

"Private investigator. How do you not know what that is?" He looked around and nodded. "I guess this place is even more in the sticks than I thought."

"I know what a PI is, I didn't know people actually used them." I shrugged. "What are you meeting with him for? I don't think he'll be able to help you with this. Everything you need should be right in there." I pointed to the building behind me.

"I'm not meeting with him for that. Although, it might not hurt to see what he can dig up." Silas slid his phone back in his pocket. "What did you want to see me about?"

"If you're not seeing him for all this, then what? How much could a kid your age possibly need to know?"

Silas shook his head and smirked. "Is everyone in this town like you?"

"What does that even mean?"

"People around here are nosy."

"We're nosy? Says the kid who hired a PI. That's next level nosy." I smirked. "Do you have a few minutes? There's some things I want to talk to you about before you head home."

"I'm not going anywhere." Silas nudged his head in the direction of the park bench. "Is over there okay?"

"Sure." I took deep breaths with every step as I made my way to the bench.

Silas motioned for me to sit before he joined me. "So, what is it that you want to talk about?"

147

"I'm not sure where to start." I tightened my grip on my purse strap. "My dad's sick."

"I heard." Silas turned to face me. "I'm sorry."

"Thanks." I swallowed the words I wanted to say. "He's having a hard time with this case being opened."

"Why's that?" Silas put his hands between his legs.

"Well, I think it's because it was one of the biggest cases he worked on. He spent so many hours here trying to get to the bottom of it. And now, he feels like someone is looking over his shoulder. Like he didn't know how to do his job."

"I don't understand why he'd feel that way. Shouldn't he want the case to be closed? If he worked so hard to bring justice to my father, wouldn't this be what he wants?"

"No, it's not like that. By opening this up it undermines everything he ever did. It's like his whole career was a joke. You see how small this town is, where we're all nosy? People talk."

Silas nodded. "And you don't want it getting back to your dad?"

"Right, although he already thinks the gossip has started." I lifted my shoulders. "And he's probably right. There's nothing better to do around here."

"But what's the big deal if people talk? If your dad did his best, they'll see that when they go through the files. Technology has changed, anything that's found this time doesn't mean he missed it. It wasn't the man, but the equipment."

I sighed. "That's not how things work around here. It won't matter that he didn't have the tools, what will matter is that he'll be made a fool of." I rubbed my forehead. "He's dying. I don't know how much longer he has."

"I had no idea." Silas leaned forward. "How about I call off the investigation until your dad... uh... passes?"

DEPENDING ON YOU

"You'd do that?" I covered my mouth. "Oh my god, that would be such a big relief."

"Okay." Silas smiled. "See, problem solved."

"You don't know what this means to me. What can I do to repay you?"

"That's not necessary." Silas stood up and pulled out his phone. "Well, actually, there is one thing I could use some help with."

"Anything." I rolled my shoulders to push out the lingering tension.

"You grew up here, right?"

"That's right." I walked with him back to our cars.

"Would you be willing to help me find my birth mother?"

"Sure, I'd be happy to help." I took a folded-up envelope out of my purse and dug around for a pen. "What do you know so far?"

"Not much." Silas shrugged. "That's why I'm meeting with the PI. What I do know is it was a closed adoption and my parents worked with an agency out of Vermont. I was born on March 23, 1999."

"Alright." I wrote the information down. "Do you know the name of the agency?"

"Pine Grove Family Planning Center. They're not in business any longer, that's why I'm hoping we can find someone who used to work there that might remember something."

"You want me to help you find them?" I held my pen in my hand. "I'm not sure I'd even know where to start."

Silas shook his head. "Since you're from here, I'd like you to ask around about my father. From what I can tell he was living here at the time of his death. Someone must have known him. If

149

you can find out who his friends were, then they might know who my mother is."

"Okay." I put the information back into my purse and unlocked my door. "It's been twenty years, though. I'm not sure anyone will remember."

"It's not like there are a ton of murders in this town. I'm sure if people knew him, they'd remember something. If not," he shrugged, "then at least I know we tried."

"Okay. I will do my best to help you."

"What's your number? I'll text you mine, so you'll have it." Silas turned on his phone and entered my number. My purse vibrated when I received the text.

"Got it." I tapped my purse. "Thank you." I placed my hand on my chest. "Good luck at your meeting. I hope you find some answers."

"Me, too." Silas waved before walking away. "Give your dad my best."

"I will." With my hands firmly on the steering wheel I rested my head on my seat. If I couldn't take responsibility for my actions at least I could help. Not quite the same, but at least I might be able to answer some of his questions and relieve some of my guilt.

Chapter Twenty-Seven

PATTI

"Was there any evidence when you worked that case?" I cleared my throat. "I mean, was there anything that could be linked back to the killer?"

"Not a thing." Mr. Silver rubbed his chin. "And there sure as hell won't be anything now. I'm the one that carried the box down to the basement. It was pretty much near empty. That kid's not going to find anything."

"But if he did," I sat on the edge of his bed, "would they be able to tell what happened all these years later?"

Mr. Silver put his hand on mine. "No. It's the coldest cold case I've ever seen." His smile lifted his glasses. "Whoever did it has nothing to worry about."

I covered his hand with mine. "I'm sorry I've been away for so long. I wish I had come home more often."

"Life happens. I know that better than anyone." He leaned his head back. "What matters is that you're here now."

My lips quivered. "But I should have been here for my mom. I let her down."

151

"No, that's not true at all. Your kids needed you. She knew that." He reached for my hand. "I spent a lot of time with your mom, she was probably my best friend." His eyes glistened. "We talked about a lot of things, and she never once said she was disappointed in you. She was so proud of you."

I brushed the tears off my cheek. "I didn't know how sick she was."

"I know. She wanted it that way. She didn't want you to worry about her. She was in good hands. Cate and I took turns taking care of her. She was comfortable and loved."

"Thank you." I sniffled. "I feel better knowing she wasn't alone."

"You're never alone when you have family." Mr. Silver rubbed my back. "She did want me to give you something." He pointed to the desk. "It's in the top drawer."

I pulled it open and saw my mom's handwriting on an envelope on top of the pile. "This?" I held it up for him to see.

"Yup, that's it." He nodded.

I returned to the bed to open it. "What's this?" I looked to Mr. Silver for answers.

"Your mom didn't want you to know about this until you were ready. And by the sounds of things, it might be time. Besides, I'm running out of time." Mr. Silver covered his mouth and coughed. "When your mom first got sick, she came to me with a check. She asked me to put it in the bank and hold on to it for you."

"Why would she do that?" I scanned the document. "I don't understand what this is."

"She never cared for Danny. She didn't want you to know, but she had a feeling you may need some money that he didn't have access to. She knew if it were in her bank account when she died, your husband would be able to spend it and if you got divorced, he'd get at least half of it."

"I knew she didn't like him." I slapped my knee and laughed. "She'd never come out and tell me, but I could tell."

"To be fair, I don't really like the guy, either." Mr. Silver grinned. "Anyway, this money is yours. The only stipulation is that you don't put it in your name, at least not until your divorce is finalized or cash it and put it some place safe."

"Who said I'm getting divorced?" I raised my brow.

"I'm dying, I'm not deaf." He chuckled. "I heard you and Cate talking. If you're not, you should consider it." He put his hand on my arm. "You're too good of a girl to be treated that way. You deserve all of his love, not just the pieces he has left over."

I nodded as I held back the tears. "It's not what I expected."

"It never is." He shook his head. "Linda was a piece of work. I never knew who was going to be in my bed if I came home early, or if the kids were going to be fed dinner. I should have done better for my girls, but I loved her. I wanted to fix her and have the perfect, happy little family. Instead, I got a broken heart and two daughters with abandonment issues."

"You were a good dad, don't feel like her mistakes were your fault. Cate and Sammy love you so much." I took his hand. "You've always been like a dad to me. After my dad died, you were always there for me. I'll never forget that."

"It's what family does." He smiled. "Maybe you could move back here. Bring your kids. I know Cate would love that."

The paper crinkled in my hand. "I can't believe Mom did this for me. It opens up so many possibilities for us."

"That's what she wanted. I'm sorry I held on to it for as

long as I did. I wasn't sure how to get it to you without Danny knowing, and I didn't know things had gotten so bad for you."

"No, this is perfect timing." I rubbed my finger over my mother's handwriting and was encased with warmth. "I'll be sure to make her proud."

"Too late, you already have. Me, too." Mr. Silver's eyes sparkled. "I'm going to make the check out to Cate, that way there won't be any trace of it in case you decide to get divorced. Screw the bastard."

"Is there anything I can do for you? Any pressing bucket list items you want to cross off?" I lifted my shoulders. "Like jump out of a plane or something?"

"Funny you should ask. There is one thing I'd like to do." Mr. Silver rubbed his chin.

"What is it?" I folded the paper back up and gave him my full attention.

"Not yet." He closed his eyes. "I'm tired right now, but I'll let you know when I'm ready."

Chapter Twenty-Eight

CATE

Patti and Sammy were sitting on the front porch when I pulled into the driveway. I blew out the resentment that had been festering and put on a smile before getting out of the car. "Hey guys."

"You look surprisingly cheerful." Patti twisted her lips and held her mug to her mouth. "How did it go?"

"Very well." I sat on the arm of Patti's chair. "Nice to see you two catching up."

"Sammy was telling me about her new boyfriend." Patti set her empty cup down.

I stopped myself from rolling my eyes and nodded. "That's nice."

"I was telling Patti that I'm going to bring him over. Maybe for dinner." Sammy stood up and brushed off her legs. "I'm going to go see if Dad needs anything."

I bit the inside of my cheek and waited for her to walk away. "You've got to be kidding me."

"Oh, come on. She's happy." Patti patted my arm. "And she's hurting, too. Losing your dad is going to be hard on her."

155

"I know. She just has a way of getting under my skin. Every time she speaks, it's like nails on a chalkboard." I got up and took over Sammy's chair.

"So, what happened?" Patti crossed her legs before leaning back.

"I met him." I looked up at the oak tree's branches hanging over the porch roof. "He's a good kid."

"Really? You figured that out in the little time you two spent together?"

"Yeah, I did." The smile spread across my face. "He's going to call off the investigation, at least until Dad... you know, dies."

Patti turned her head and narrowed her eyes. "Why would he do that?"

"I asked him to." I lifted my shoulders. "I explained how upset it would make Dad if the case was solved while he was still alive. He said he understood and said he'd stop digging, at least for now."

"Wow, that's amazing." Patti leaned forward and stretched. "I can't believe you were able to convince him to hold off for now."

"All I have to do is help him find his birth mother." I rested my head on the back of the chair and let the sun warm my face. "He's with a PI right now."

"A PI? He's working with an investigator?" Patti sneered. "I can't believe the entitlement of this generation."

"What are you talking about?" I raised my brow. "He's practically the same age as Sammy and you're all into her going after what she wants."

"It seems... I don't know, pretentious that because this kid has money, he can track down anybody he wants." Patti folded her arms. "It's not right."

DEPENDING ON YOU

"Why is this upsetting you so much? Silas wants to find out where he came from. His father didn't turn out the way he hoped, thanks to me and now he wants to find the woman who gave him life. It's the least I can do for the poor kid."

"Yeah, I guess. It just seems wrong. Don't you think his mother would have stayed in touch if she wanted to?" Patti pushed the hair off her shoulder and sighed. "But if it makes you feel better at least let me help."

"It doesn't sound like you really want to." I pulled the envelope with the information Silas had given me out of my purse.

"I do. It's just a lot all at once."

"Silas was born March 23, 1999 and placed for adoption at the Pine Grove Adoption Agency in Stark County. It was a closed adoption and the agency has closed." I looked up at Patti who was chewing her fingernail.

"He knows quite a bit already. If he's working with a PI, why does he need your help?" Patti asked.

"He wants me to ask around town and see if anyone knew Trevor. Since he was living in town at the time of his death, Silas thinks someone around here might know who Trevor was dating."

"Don't you think someone would have mentioned something by now if they knew anything? Lawrenceville is a small town. If there was any thought Trevor could have had a baby, don't you think it would have been spread like wildfire through this place?" Patti tapped her foot. "It won't hurt to ask. And if I find his mother, maybe he won't demand to have the investigation started again." I rubbed my eyes. "It might be the only way I don't end up behind bars."

"But why would his mother bring him to Stark County if she were from here? That part doesn't add up." Patti shifted in

157

her seat. "Stark County is at least six hours from here. Why would anyone drive that far to put their baby up for adoption?"

"I don't know. Maybe she didn't want anyone to know. Maybe she moved out there after she found out she was pregnant. Or she might have family over there." I studied all the facts I had. "Anything is possible, including her being from here. I told Silas I'd ask around and that's what I'm going to do."

"Fair enough." Patti nodded. "We can work on this together. Divide and conquer."

"Thanks." I tapped my lip. "I have some ideas where to start but I want to think it over more."

"Alright. Whenever you're ready let me know." Patti stood up and stretched. "I think I'm going to call Katie and Logan and check in. God only knows what kind of mischief those two could be up to."

"Oh, I think we have a pretty good idea." I smirked. "We got into our fair share of trouble."

"Don't remind me." Patti covered her face. "I'm not ready to think about them getting into the trouble we did. The world was a different place back when we were kids."

"Was it? Or were we too naïve to notice? I'm sure there was just as much messed up stuff going on all around us when we were their age."

"I'm not so sure about that. It was a simpler time. We weren't always available on social media. If we wanted to ditch someone, we didn't answer the phone. Now the kids have little maps that shows everyone where they are. Except me, of course. I'm far too uncool to be let into that secret alliance." Patti snickered. "I'm so glad we weren't prisoners to our devices back then."

DEPENDING ON YOU

"Right. It was so much better when we were just prisoners to our minds." I tucked the envelope back in my purse and followed Patti inside to get started on operation interrogate the neighborhood.

Chapter Twenty-Nine
PATTI

Who could have known Trevor? The thought played on repeat in my mind as I rested on the couch next to Mr. Silver. None of his friends or family came forward when he died. It was easier to assume he wasn't missed. I'd never noticed him around town before the accident.

"Are you up?" Mr. Silver's voice broke the silence in the room. "Patti?"

"Yeah, what do you need?" I flung my feet to the floor and sat up.

"Nothing really. I couldn't sleep and didn't know if you wanted to keep me company." Mr. Silver lifted his head. "Can you help me sit up?"

I fumbled around his bed until I found the remote. "Is that good?" I held my finger over the button.

"A little more." He flashed a patient smile. "That's perfect."

I turned on the lamp and sat on the side of his bed. "How are you feeling?"

Mr. Silver shrugged. "Ah. As good as can be expected." He

160

DEPENDING ON YOU

cleared his throat. "I'm more concerned with how you're doing."

"Me?" I pointed to my chest. "I'm fine."

"Come on, you can talk to me. It's not like I'll tell anyone. I might die before I get the chance." He chuckled. "Sorry, it sounded better in my head. It seems like something is bothering you. I know you've got a lot on your mind."

"No, I'm fine." I bit my bottom lip to keep it from quivering. "I'm glad I'm here with you and the girls. It's nice to be home."

"Patti." Mr. Silver twisted his mouth. "I know there's more going on than what you and Catie are telling me."

"I don't know what you're talking about." I smoothed out the blanket next to me. "Everything's fine. We're fine. There's nothing you need to worry about."

Mr. Silver tilted his head. "So, you're not going to tell me?" He closed his eyes and took a deep breath.

My heart jumped into my throat. "What do you mean?"

"I'll be here when you're ready to talk, but I can't promise you how much longer I have." Mr. Silver held out his hand. "You know there's nothing you or Catie could do that would make me think less of you."

I nodded and sucked back the emotion brewing inside. "I know. You're a good man, Mr. Silver."

"I do have one favor to ask." He held up his index finger.

"Sure, anything you need." I pushed the hair out of my face.

"Can you make sure that after I'm gone, people don't turn me into a saint? I don't want to be put on any pedestal. I had my faults and I want to make sure people remember those, too."

"Okay." I pushed up a half smile. "But then you've got to do some stuff for us to talk about."

161

"Oh, honey, there's plenty." He closed his eyes. "I've done more than my fair share of stuff I wished I hadn't." He took my hand in his. "But haven't we all?"

"That's for sure." My shoulders rose and fell as I emptied my lungs. "Is there anything you'd like to get off your chest? Something you don't want to bring with you?"

Mr. Silver nodded. "Yeah, there's a couple things, but I'm not ready yet."

"Well, when you are, let me know. It can be our secret if it makes it easier."

"Thank you." He gave my hand a squeeze before letting it go. "Do you believe in Heaven?"

"I do. The only thing that helped me after my dad died was believing he was in a better place. I think about my mom and dad back together and sometimes I wish I could be with them." I looked away as the tears welled up in my eyes. "I envy you."

"Oh, Patti. Don't. You have so much of your life left to live. The problem is you're not living. Do me and them a favor and find something that brings you joy. The world is too ugly of a place to not have something to look forward to."

"I'm trying." I rubbed my eyes. "But I don't even know what I should be looking for."

"You'll know when you find it." Mr. Silver smiled and placed his hand on his chest. "And you'll feel it."

"What if I had it once but I let it go? What if I can't ever get it back again?"

"Then it wasn't meant for you. When it's meant to be, it'll all fall into place. You won't have to wonder. You'll just know." Mr. Silver put his hand on my back. "Just like you and Catie."

"I got lucky with her. There's never been anyone that compares to her."

DEPENDING ON YOU

"See, that's what you're looking for." Mr. Silver put his head down and closed his eyes. "I'm going to try to get a little more rest."

I went into the kitchen and poured two glasses of wine and went to Cate's room. There was enough moonlight to see the outline of her under the covers. I stood and watched as the sheets rose and fell with her breath. The door creaked when I turned to walk away.

"Who's there?" Cate's arm reached out from under the sheet. The glow of a phone lit up her face.

"It's me. I brought wine." I handed her a glass as I stood by her bedside.

"Wine? What time is it?" She turned her phone over. "It's two in the morning. What are you doing up?"

"I couldn't sleep." I sat next to her and took a sip.

"Yeah, me either." Cate turned the lamp on. "I keep trying to figure out what I'm going to do about Silas. I've already made a list of the people I need to talk to, but what if no one is willing to help me? What if I don't find him enough answers before..."

"He told you he was going to wait. Believe him until he gives you a reason not to." I put my hand on her knee. "We'll work together. I'll take some of the names and we can split the work up."

"What happens if I find his mother and she doesn't want to be found? Do I sell her out just to save myself?"

"One thing at a time. Let's find her first and then we can ask questions." I emptied my glass. "Are you going to drink that?"

"No."

I took her glass and emptied that, too. "We can start in the

163

morning." I lifted the sheet and nestled myself in. "It's okay if I sleep with you, right?"

Cate laughed. "You look pretty comfortable, so who am I to tell you no?"

"I've missed this. It's been too long since we've had a sleepover."

"It has been." Cate joined me, placing her arm around me. "I don't know what I'd do without you. You're the best."

"You've done just fine without me." I squeezed my eyes closed. "I've been a terrible friend. I'm going to do everything I can to make it up to you."

"Don't be crazy. I'm the one who ruined your life. If it weren't for me, you never would have left. I know how bad I screwed things up. I'm lucky you still want to be part of my life."

"I'm the lucky one." I sucked back the tears and let the wine lull me to sleep.

Chapter Thirty
CATE

"This is impossible." I tossed the notebook across the kitchen table. "How am I supposed to find any of these people? It's not like we were friends with Trevor's friends." I rested my elbows on the table and held my face.

"Look on Facebook." Patti took a drink of coffee. "Here, give me a name to look up." She turned on her phone.

"Facebook? Are you kidding me?" I leaned my head back. "I want to find them. I don't want them to find me."

"Cate, you're not serious, right? You live in the same house in the same town you grew up in. If people wanted to find you, they could." She set her mug down and picked up the notebook. "Watch this." She typed something into her phone. "Look, Richard Hulls lives in Murray, New Hampshire."

"You found someone already?" I took her phone and scrolled through the results. "How did you do that?"

"It's easy. Do you want me to help you sign up for an account? That way you can send them messages. It might be easier than trying to call them." Patti reached for her phone and

165

typed something in before handing it back to me. "Here you go."

"Oh my god, Patti." I covered my mouth. "He's as cute as I remembered him."

"He doesn't live that far from here, why don't you start by sending him a message?" Patti wiggled her eyebrows.

"I don't have time for that." I clicked on his picture and enlarged it on the screen. "The years have been kind to him. I'm sure he can do better than me."

"Knock it off. He's still in love with you. He never stopped. I told you we talk, and most of those talks revolve around you." Patti leaned over me and pushed her finger across the screen. "Look."

"Oh my god." I clicked on the link. "Jake posted *Because You Loved Me* on my birthday. That was our song."

"Yeah, I know. He posts that song every year, and sometimes when he drinks too much, he adds little comments." Patti laughed. "He usually takes them down when he sobers up. It's probably why his wife left him."

"He's never forgotten me?" I handed Patti back her phone. "Why didn't you tell me before?"

"I didn't want to make you feel guilty. Plus, I didn't want to get Jake's hopes up. He can't take losing you again. He barely survived the first time." Patti returned to her seat. "Why don't you make yourself an account and see if he remembers anything from that summer? You know, besides all the fun you two love-birds had."

"He was my first and my last." I picked at my fingernail. "I've never gotten over him, either."

"Then what are you waiting for? Life's so short. Don't

166

DEPENDING ON YOU

waste it being miserable." Patti put her hand out. "Give me your phone."

"Why?" I held it above her hand. "What are you going to do?"

"I'm going to download the app and help you get some friends." Patti's cheeks lifted. "And then, you're going to put some effort into making yourself happy."

"No, I can't." I fidgeted in my chair. "I..."

"You what? Don't deserve happiness?" Patti avoided eye contact. "That's bullshit. Just like it's bullshit that I don't deserve it. We've paid our dues, Cate. We shouldn't have to pay for the rest of our lives."

"You're not the one who took a man's life. I am. People like me don't get happily ever afters." I pushed myself away from the table.

"Cate, that's not true." Her voice softened. "Have you ever thought you're not only punishing yourself, but all the people who love you, too? Look at Jake, he wants to be with you more than anything. He has for the last twenty years and the poor guy keeps waiting. You're who he wants. But he has to live with his ache inside of himself because the woman he loves hates herself so much that she's willing to spend the rest of her life alone than give into an ounce of happiness."

"That's not fair." My face burned as her words sunk in. "You have no idea what it's like to live in this hell. Every day I wait for something bad to happen because I know it's going to. Every single day I look over my shoulder waiting for someone to slap handcuffs on me. No one else deserves to live in this prison with me. Jake is better off without me. And it's because I love him that I stay away." I sucked in air before I began to sob. "I don't want to live like this anymore, Patti."

167

She came over and held me close. "I know." She stroked my hair as I fell to pieces in her arms. "I know."

"I need to tell someone." I pulled my head off her chest. "I can't keep this secret forever."

"Cate." She closed her eyes and leaned her head back. "What about your dad? He needs you with him, remember? That's why you're helping Silas." She pushed the hair out of my face. "Can't it wait? At least a little bit longer?"

"I don't think it can. It's killing me." My shoulders fell. "I'm so tired, Patti."

"I know. Me, too." Patti took my hands. "Let me help you find Silas's mother and then we can confess."

"I do owe it to him. It's the least I can do for the poor kid. But as soon as I get him the information, I have to..."

"Okay. That sounds fair." Patti braced herself on the counter and took a deep breath. "Why don't you call Silas and see if we can meet with him? If we get the information he has we can make better use of our time. No use in looking under the same rock."

"Thanks, Patti, for understanding and for not leaving me." I wiped away my tears. "I don't mean to be impossible to be around. I want to do better for the people who love me."

"We're a team, remember?" She picked the notebook and her phone off the table. "Let me do some research while you take a shower. Then we can see if Silas has time to meet with us."

I blew Patti a kiss. "You're too good to me." I had to believe I was worthy of her love. We fit too well together not to be. The sooner I get this off my chest, the sooner everything else will fall into place. I can feel it.

168

Chapter Thirty-One

PATTI

The house was just how I remembered it. Mom's gardens were blooming with the same flowers that covered the lawn for as long as I could remember. "Do you know them?" I pulled the car over in front of the home I grew up in.

"No. No one knows their neighbors anymore. That died along with our childhood." Cate's cheeks turned up. "We had so much fun in there."

"We sure did." I blinked my eyes to push back the pain. "I miss it."

"What part?" Cate asked, still focused on the home in front of us.

"All of it. I miss my parents and my old room. I miss my mom's cooking and my dad's jokes." I took a tissue out of my purse and blew my nose. "I'd do anything to have one more day with them."

Cate frowned. "I'm sorry, Patti. I wish I could give that to you."

"Thank you for taking care of her." I put the car in drive

and pulled back on to the road. "Don't worry, I'm not mad. Your dad told me what you guys did for her."

"I should have called you." Cate twisted her ring. "I didn't know what to do. She didn't want you to worry and I didn't want to believe she was as sick as she was."

"She loved you like a daughter. You and Sammy. Thank you for being there for her when I couldn't." I tapped my fingers on the steering wheel.

"I loved her, too. She really helped keep me together while you were gone. I told her the truth about that night." Cate cleared her throat. "She..."

"You told her?" I tightened my grip on the wheel. "Why did you do that?"

"Something in me needed to apologize for keeping you away. I needed her to know it wasn't her keeping you away." Cate turned her head away from me.

"What did she say?"

"It was one of our last conversations, after she couldn't talk anymore. She squeezed my hand, so I know she heard me." Cate covered her face. "I know I should have told you."

"No, it's okay. I'm glad she knew." I leaned my head against the seat. "Do you know what he drives?" I pulled into the library's parking lot.

She pointed to the only car in the lot. "He's right there."

I studied the boy leaned up against the black Dodge Charger. "My god, he looks like he should be on a GQ cover."

"He is a handsome tyke, isn't he?" Cate hit my arm. "We're old enough to be his mother."

"I was just going to say that. He's only two years older than Logan." I reached into the back seat to get my purse. "Come on, let's go see what he found out."

DEPENDING ON YOU

"Hi Silas." Cate stood between us. "This is my best friend, Patti. She's offered to help us, if that's okay with you."

"Of course." Silas smiled. "The more the merrier."

I extended my hand. "It's nice to meet you."

"You as well." Silas nodded. "I'm glad you called me. I was able to get some information yesterday that should help at least point me in the right direction."

"Really? Already? That's exciting." Cate walked with Silas into the library, while I trailed behind.

"Yeah, I wasn't expecting much, but this guy had some connections." Silas took off his backpack and set it on the floor before sitting down.

"He had connections?" I tilted my head as I struggled to keep what I was thinking off my face.

"Yup. He knew a guy that knew someone who worked at the adoption agency." Silas pulled his laptop out of his bag.

"But Vermont is a closed adoption state. How can they violate someone's wishes like that?" I folded my hands in front of me. "I mean, I'm glad you're getting your answers, but maybe there was a reason it was closed."

Silas narrowed his eyes. "Vermont isn't a closed record state, it's a partial closed record state, which means if there is a good reason to open the records, then you can."

"And this is a good reason?" I rolled my neck between my shoulders. "Well, I guess you're in luck then."

"The real problem is that the adoption agency closed a few years after I was born, and most likely destroyed all of the records." Silas ran his fingers through his hair.

"Why would they destroy the records?" Cate sat on the edge of her chair. "That doesn't make sense. Shouldn't they keep those things forever?"

171

"Pine Grove appears to have been breaking multiple laws. Before they shut their doors, they destroyed everything, most likely trying to cover up the fraud." Silas turned around his computer to show us the screen. "This page is for victims of Pine Grove. This is where birth parents and adoptees can connect with each other."

"So, if your birth mother is looking for you, she'd be on here?" I squinted to look at the screen. "What if she doesn't know about it?"

"The guy said if she did a search online, she'd find it. And if she's not looking for me, the guy who used to work at Pine Grove might know where to find the person in charge of my adoption. We're waiting to hear back from him." Silas pulled his computer back in front of him and started typing.

"If they don't have any of the records, how would they know who the person in charge of your adoption was?" Cate peered over Silas's shoulder. "Wouldn't that have been lost, too?"

"The guy said he was confident he remembers the case. I was the only boy given up that spring. All the other babies were girls." Silas shrugged. "I don't want to get my hopes up. I'll wait and see what they find out."

"That seems fishy." Cate held her chin in her hand as she leaned on the table. "You were the only boy given up for adoption? Are you paying this guy for the information? It seems like he's making it up."

"I'm not paying him, but the PI might be. I don't see what good lying would do. It's not like he guaranteed he'll find her." Silas closed his laptop. "I've waited this long, what's a few more days?"

DEPENDING ON YOU

"How long have you known you were adopted?" I rubbed my hand over the smooth tabletop.

"I always knew." Silas put his computer back in his backpack. "But my parents didn't officially tell me until I turned eighteen."

"What do you mean you always knew? Did your parents treat you badly?" I looked into his hazel eyes searching for any sign of pain.

"No, they've been great. It wasn't anything they did wrong. It was just this feeling I had since I can remember that I wasn't theirs. Maybe it's because they're older. I don't really know."

"Do you have siblings?" I twirled my hair around my finger.

"No, I'm an only child. That's another reason I wanted to find my birth parents. I've always wanted a brother or sister to share my life with. I'll be alone after my parents are gone."

"You didn't miss out on anything spectacular." Cate rolled her eyes. "Trust me."

"Don't listen to her." I laughed. "I'm an only child, too, and I always wanted someone to grow old with."

"Do you have kids?" Silas asked as he looked between us.

"Nope, that ship has sailed for me." Cate tapped her fingers on the table.

"I have two." I took my phone out of my purse. "This is Logan, he's seventeen and that's Katie, she's sixteen."

Silas studied the picture. "Wow, they're really close in age."

"Yeah, I wanted to make sure they had each other. I didn't want to risk waiting too long. You never know what life will throw at you." I flipped through the pictures. "I hope you find what you're looking for. No one deserves to live this life alone."

"I guess she's right." Cate scoffed. "It is nice to have someone to lean on, even if they are ultra-annoying and needy."

'Sammy's a good kid. I remember how special she was to you. I know it will all even out eventually. Give the girl some time." I slid my phone back into my purse.

'Who's Sammy?" Silas asked.

'She's my baby sister. And by baby, I mean she's twenty-three, but she acts like a damn baby." Cate snickered. 'I'm kidding." She held her hands up. 'I know I should be thankful to have her in my life."

Silas laughed. 'I guess there are some perks to being an only child. Even if I don't have any siblings, I at least want to know. Wondering is so much harder than knowing."

"That's the truth." I nodded. 'We'll do whatever it takes to get you answers."

"Thanks." Silas smiled. 'Have you found anyone who knew my father yet?"

'I have a list of people I'm going to ask. Patti had the great idea to reach out to them on Facebook."

"That's a good idea. Most old people have a profile on there." Silas leaned back in his chair. 'That's not what I meant. I don't mean you're old. I mean the people who knew my father will be."

'Well, smarty pants, I don't even have an account yet. This old lady over here is going to help me get one." Cate pointed in my direction.

'You guys aren't old. My parents are. My dad will be seventy in a couple of months." Silas smirked. 'Even he has Facebook."

'I'll have one by the end of the day." Cate crossed her arms. 'And I'll start sending the messages, as soon as I figure it all out."

'It's simple. You might even like it." Silas stretched. 'I'm

DEPENDING ON YOU

kind of hungry. Do you ladies want to go get something to eat with me?"

"I have to get home to help Sammy with my dad." Cate looked at me with widened eyes.

"Do you want to order a couple of pizzas and come back to Cate's house with us?" I either still have what it takes to read Cate's signals, or I failed miserably. Time will tell.

Chapter Thirty-Two

CATE

Sammy held her finger to her lips when we opened the door. She pushed us back outside, where she joined us. "He's not doing good. I had to give him some more morphine." She folded her arms and looked up. "I'm not ready for this, Cate. He can't die."

"How could he have gotten so sick so fast? Are you sure you weren't just trying to get him to go to sleep so you could get out of here?" I moved her out of the way of the door.

Silas put his hand on my shoulder. "Take it easy on her."

I swung my head around to scold him when I saw the softness in his eyes. "Fine." I blew out the resentment and turned back to Sammy. "I'm sorry."

"I don't know why you hate me so much." Sammy's body heaved as she sobbed. "Where's Patti and who's this?"

"Patti's getting pizza for us, and this is Silas." I took a step closer to her and put my hand on her arm. "I don't hate you. I'm just under a lot of pressure right now."

"You're under a lot of pressure?" She swatted my hand off

176

DEPENDING ON YOU

her. "Do you think you're the only one? God, it's always about you."

"What? When is it ever about me? Sorry if I didn't want to become a mom at fourteen when Mom decided she was going to whore around while Dad went to work." Adrenaline coursed through my veins as years of resentment came to the surface. "You have no idea what you're talking about."

"Don't bring Mom into this. You're an awful person. I wish it were you in there dying and not Dad." Sammy went inside and slammed the door.

"Welcome to my lovely abode." I held my hand out. "See, this is why you're lucky you're an only child."

"I can go." Silas ran his hand through his hair. "It seems like you two have some things to discuss."

"No, it's always like this." I held my hand out for him to take. "I'll do my best to behave. Besides, Patti keeps me in line."

"Are you sure? I don't want to get in the way."

Patti pulled into the driveway. "Looks like you're stuck here now."

"What's going on? Is everything okay?" Patti got out of the car and joined us on the porch.

"Everything's fine. Sammy and I exchanged a few words, but we're good now." I smiled.

"In front of Silas?" Patti shook her head. "Come on, you girls can do better than this. Your dad needs you two to work together. You don't want him to feel guilty for dying."

My shoulders fell with a sigh. "See, told you Patti would keep us in line."

"I'm serious. You two need to figure out how to get along." Patti bent down and pulled out three large boxes of pizza. "Let's have some lunch and try to cool down."

177

Dad's eyes were open, staring at the ceiling when I got inside. "Did you get it out of your system?"

"I'm sorry, Dad. I didn't mean…"

"Yes, you did." He turned his head and nodded. "I know I've made some mistakes."

"No, that's not what I said." I inched closer to his bed. "I know you did your best."

"Catie, I screwed up. I put too much weight on your shoulders. I should have known better. If I had stepped up, you could have lived your own life. I know how much you gave up for me." He closed his eyes. "Thank you for everything. We couldn't have done it without you."

"Dad." I sat on the edge of his bed. "You're not the reason I gave everything up."

Patti handed the pizza boxes to Silas and widened her eyes and shook her head. "You're a great father, Mr. Silver. You did your best, and that's all anyone could have ever asked for. Your girls are who they are because of you. Don't beat yourself up over things you can't change. They love you, and that's all you need to know that you did a good job."

A tear ran down Dad's cheek. "I don't want you to resent your sister. It's not her fault, any more than it is yours. We were dealt a shitty hand, but not all of the cards were bad." A smile replaced his frown.

"Mr. Silver?" Patti cleared her throat. "I want to introduce you to someone." She took the pizzas from Silas and handed them to me.

Dad turned his head and squinted. "Who's there?"

"Silas Tanner, sir." Silas extended his hand.

"You're that kid stirring up all the dust in town?" Dad lifted

DEPENDING ON YOU

his head. "What do you want now? To spit on me before they put me in the ground?"

"Dad, I invited him here." I set the boxes on the coffee table. "Patti and I are helping him."

"Are you out of your mind?" Dad fumbled with his bed remote.

I elevated his head so he could sit up. "No, Dad, Silas is a nice guy. He's not from here and we want to help him find his birth mother. You always taught us to lend a hand when we can, so we are."

"I don't mean any disrespect sir. I wasn't trying to say you didn't know how to do your job. I just wanted to see if there was anything new that could have developed over the years."

"Why? Your father was the biggest piece of shit I knew." Dad coughed into his hand. "The world became a better place the night he died."

"You knew him?" Silas crossed his hands in front of him.

"Yeah, we all knew him down at the station. He wasn't a good person. He hurt everyone he came in contact with. You're lucky he didn't get the chance to destroy you." Color returned to Dad's cheeks for the first time in days as he spoke of the dead man.

"I didn't know you knew him." I looked over at Patti. She was staring off into space. I couldn't summon her attention.

"It's a small town. Everyone knew him." Dad rolled his eyes. "If you didn't score your drugs off the scumbag, he probably robbed you."

"I had no idea what type of man he was." Silas put his hands behind his head and looked up. "I shouldn't have come here and made a mess of things."

179

"The damage is done. Now all his victims get to have their trauma dug up all because someone with no clue was trying to get him justice. It's a damn shame." Dad took a deep breath. "Even if you wanted to put an end to the whole mess, it's too late. Your money brought out the big guns."

Silas dropped his head. "I know. I was going to tell you..."

"So, they're not calling off the investigation?" My pulse throbbed against my neck. I braced myself on the wall as the realization of what was about took my breath away.

"No." Silas sighed. "I asked them to hold off but once the team opened the case back up, they weren't willing to shut it back down. I had no idea. I swear."

"And you weren't going to tell me? You were going to let me help you find your birth mother and not tell me that you didn't keep your end of the deal?" I clenched my fists and waited for Patti to stop me from saying something I shouldn't. She didn't even make eye contact with me.

"What kind of deal are you talking about?" Dad lifted his head off the pillow. "Cate, what are you talking about?"

"It's nothing, Dad. Don't worry about it." I stormed past Silas and slammed the door behind me. Outside in the fresh air I tried to find a solution to fix this mess. There was nothing I could do. I paced the yard as I thought about my options. If I confessed now, maybe they'd let me stay out of jail long enough to take care of Dad. Or maybe I could convince Patti to stay with Dad until he dies. There was no way Sammy could handle it on her own.

I pulled at my hair and screamed until my throat was raw. I fell to the ground and curled up into a ball. This was not how it was supposed to happen.

DEPENDING ON YOU

"Catie, what's wrong?" Sammy's soft voice lulled me out of the tunnel of rage I was descending into.

"Everything." I hid my head under my arms and sobbed.

"What's going on? Why is Patti crying?" Sammy pushed the hair out of my face. "Why are you crying?"

I lifted my head out of the dirt to look at Sammy. "Patti's crying?"

"Yeah, she's in the bathroom. She wouldn't let me in. And that guy's sitting by himself in the kitchen."

I sat up and wiped off my face. "She won't talk to you?"

"No, she won't open the door, either." Sammy took my hand and helped me up. "What happened? Is this because of our fight?"

"No, it has nothing to do with you." I closed my eyes and took a deep breath. "Silas is the son of that guy who was killed."

"What? Why is he here? That doesn't make any sense." Sammy followed behind me. "What's he doing here?"

I held my hand up. "Look, it's a long story, and I don't have time right now to explain."

Dad held out his hand as I walked by. "What's going on? Is there something you need to tell me?" His eyes pierced my core.

"No. Yes. Just give me a minute to find Patti." I rushed down the hall and knocked on the bathroom door. "Patti, can I come in?"

"I'll be right out." The toilet flushed and the water turned on.

"Let me in." I rested my head on the door. "Come on. Please."

I took a step back when I heard the doorknob turn. Patti pulled me into the room with her. Her eyes were bloodshot and wet. "I need to..."

181

wrapped her in a hug. "I'm sorry I dragged you into this again. I didn't expect Dad to react like that."

"It's not..."

"I'm an awful friend. I shouldn't have even gotten us involved in this mess again." I let go of Patti and squeezed my arms around myself. "I need to go to the police. I don't want you getting charged with anything, so you need to promise me that you won't tell them you were there. You know nothing. I never told you a thing."

"Cate." Patti hung her head. "Don't go. I will. I'll tell them it was me."

"Absolutely not. There's no way I'd ever let you do that. Your kids need you. There's no reason for me to even exist. I don't contribute to society. No one will miss me." I held my head. "I'll leave right now."

"No, don't do that. We need to talk." Patti sat on the edge of the tub. "Your dad needs you. You can't leave him, not yet. Don't do anything until you need to. Just because the case is being investigated doesn't mean they'll ever know who did it. Your dad even said there wasn't any evidence. There's nothing to put you there. Please, think this through before you do anything."

"Okay, fine. But I at least need to tell Dad. He knows something's up. I can't lie to him." I stood in front of the mirror and stared at the reflection looking back at me. "I need him to know."

Patti blew out through her mouth. "Silas needs to leave. We can't tell him."

"Okay, I'll ask him to leave. He might have already left." I covered my face. "Poor kid."

DEPENDING ON YOU

"I'll ask him. Why don't you encourage Sammy to go out for a while, too?"

"Alright." My body trembled as I tried to gather my thoughts. I could only hope Dad would forgive me.

Chapter Thirty-Three
CATE

Patti pulled a chair close to Dad's bed and sat next to us. I stretched my arms out in front of me and took a deep breath.

"What's going on, girls?" Dad asked as he looked between us.

"I have something I need to say." I twitched my nose to hold back the tears. "I did something, and I need to tell you."

"Go on." Dad turned his head to focus on me.

"I um..." I closed my eyes and blew out my breath. "I'm the one who killed Trevor."

Dad narrowed his eyes. "What are you talking about?"

"I didn't see him." I covered my mouth as that night replayed in my mind. "I didn't know what to do. I was scared and I panicked. I know I should have told you, but I didn't want you to be disappointed with me."

"I don't understand." Dad looked to Patti. "What is she saying?"

Patti pulled out of the eye contact and lowered her head.

DEPENDING ON YOU

"Dad, I killed Trevor. It was an accident. I didn't mean to." I hid my face in my hands and rested my head on top of him.

"How'd you kill him?" Dad put his hand on my back. "What did you do?"

"I hit him with the car. I didn't see him. When I checked on him, he was already dead. I know I should have told you."

"So, you're saying you ran him over?" Dad laughed. "Catie, that was not what killed him. Why are you confessing to something you didn't do?"

"What do you mean, it wasn't what killed him? What was then?" I sat up and studied his face.

Dad shook his head. "I can't tell you that, but I can tell you that you didn't kill him."

"You don't have to cover for me. I'm ready to pay for what I did. I just wanted you to know the truth before..."

"Catie, I'm telling you, you did not kill him. There was no indication that he was hit by a car." Dad rested his head on his pillow. "I studied this case for weeks, and I can personally tell you there was nothing at the scene of the crime that will ever link you to it. You were not there. Do you understand me?"

"But I was, Dad. I need to tell you the truth." I rubbed my hand on my nose. "I can't hold on to this lie any longer."

"Is this what's taken so much of your life from you? That piece of shit stole your life, too?" Dad's body tensed. "He doesn't deserve the years he stole from you. Let it go, Catie, you are not responsible for what happened that night. Do you understand me?"

"Dad."

"No, you listen to me. There's no way I'm going to let you take the fall for this. He wasn't worth it. Whoever killed him did

185

a service for the community. Leave it at that." He held his hand up.

"I don't know if I can, Dad. If they find out I was there, I won't be able to lie. I can't live the rest of my life knowing what I did and pretending I didn't do it." I picked at his blanket. "I just needed you to know. I'm not going to tell anyone else."

"Patti, make damn sure she keeps that promise. Do not let her do anything stupid once I'm gone. I know Cate. She's a good girl and she's going to want to do what she thinks is right but trust me when I tell you that's not it."

Patti nodded. "Okay, I'll do my best."

Dad lifted his head. "I'm going to need better than that. I'm going to need a guarantee. Cate cannot take the fall for this."

"Okay." Patti picked at her fingernail. "I'll make sure." She fidgeted in her seat and kept her concentration on her hands. "I can do that because I'm the one who killed Trevor."

"Patti, I'm not going to let you take the fall for this." I rubbed my eyes. "I know you love me, and you're trying to help, but you can't keep protecting me."

Patti hung her head. "I haven't been honest with you. I wasn't protecting you. I was protecting myself."

"What are you talking about?" I pushed my hair off my shoulders.

"Cate, you didn't kill Trevor. I did. He was dead when you got to the cemetery." Patti avoided eye contact. "I wanted to tell you."

"Wait." I shot off the bed. "You're telling me you killed Trevor? And you never once thought you should say anything to me?" I clenched my fists by my side. "You let me think it was me all this time? Twenty years?"

"I didn't mean for it to go on this long." Patti looked up at me. "I've tried so many times, but..."

"When? When have you ever tried? When you moved away and ditched me? When you got to live your happily ever after, while I was stuck here pushing every good thing away? You never tried."

"Don't you think this has destroyed me, too? I wasn't brave enough to stay here and face everyone. I missed out on so much. I wasn't there when my mom needed me. I wasn't there when you needed me. I got scared, Cate." Patti's shoulders fell.

"You got scared?" I laughed. "You left me here alone to deal with it all on my own. I've never told you this, but I tried to kill myself. I wanted it all to stop. The only way I knew how was to end it all. The only reason I'm alive is because your mom found me. That's why I told her what I did. I wanted her to know I wasn't trying to leave her, like her only daughter did."

"Cate, that's enough." Dad coughed. "Hear Patti out."

"No. I never want to see her again. Get out of my house. Now," I screamed and pointed to the door, "get out!"

"Don't be like that, Cate. Patti's your best friend." Dad reached out his hand. "Don't go, Patti. You're always welcome in my house."

Patti wiped the tears out of her eyes. "She doesn't want me here. I love you, Mr. Silver." She leaned over and gave him a kiss. "I'm so sorry, for everything."

"Sorry will never give me back what I lost. I depended on you." I held the door open and waited for her to exit before slamming it shut. "You're dead to me."

Chapter Thirty-Four

PATTI

"Hey, Danny, it's me. Will you call me back as soon as you get this? I love you." I tossed my phone on the bed and buried my head in the pillow. It didn't appear that Hillside Inn had purchased any new bedding in the last twenty years. Or at least that's what it smelled like.

I rolled onto my back and counted ceiling tiles. Still thirty-four, just like the last time. Piece by piece my life was falling apart. There was no fixing what I had with Cate, and I knew it wouldn't be long before the divorce papers found me. My kids didn't need me. I doubt they'd even noticed I'm gone.

Nothing ever stays the same. Not even the parts I thought I could depend on. The parts that made me who I was. But who was I? I've been chasing the answer to that question for the past twenty years. If I'd only kept my mouth shut, I could be there for Cate right now. Except, keeping my mouth shut was what got me in this mess in the first place. The secrets were unraveling like pulling a string on a tapestry. At first no one notices the disruption, until there is a hole big enough that you can no longer ignore it.

188

DEPENDING ON YOU

The gaps within myself were too big to cover up. Running away was not an option this time because I was the one I needed to run away from. I half expected the door to open and Cate to walk in. That was in the make-believe reality I so desperately wanted to live in. Instead, I was stuck at the only hotel in Lawrenceville without a way to get home. At least not until I could get a ride to get a rental.

The last time I was here was with Cate for our sixteenth birthday. Mom rented us a room so we could celebrate in style. She stayed in the room next to us to make sure we weren't having too much fun. Cate is in every memory I have in this town. The good and the bad. There's no way I'll be able to live the rest of my life without making new memories with her.

I pulled back the curtain and saw a familiar car parked in the lot. Of course, Silas was staying here, too. There were no other options. I picked up my purse and went outside. I needed to try to find him. Ironically, he was my only hope of fixing things with Cate.

"Hey, Patti. What are you doing here?" Sammy tucked her hair behind her ear.

"More like, what are you doing here?" I raised my brow. "Is everything alright?"

She wiped her nose on her arm. "Yeah, I'm fine." She looked over her shoulder. "Don't tell Cate you saw me here, okay?"

"That shouldn't be a problem since we're not talking." I lifted my shoulders.

"What do you mean you're not talking?" Sammy scanned the area. "Come with me."

I followed behind her. "You'll have to talk with Cate. I'll let her explain."

JESSICA AIKEN-HALL

"No way. She'll never tell me anything." She sat at the picnic table. "Sit with me and tell me what's going on."

"There's nothing really to say. I messed up and Cate hates me." I blinked away the tears. "I'm going to head back home as soon as I can get a car."

"You're not going anywhere. Dad would want you here with us. Who cares what Cate wants? She's so dramatic." Sammy pushed her hair off her shoulder. "You're part of the family, too. She doesn't have the right to make you leave."

"There's a lot more to it than that. She has every right to be mad at me. There's nothing that will ever fix this." I put my purse in front of me on the table and pulled it close to me. "Why are you here? Are you in trouble?"

"I work here." Sammy shrugged.

"Like how? What do you do here?" I asked.

"It doesn't matter." She squirmed in her seat. "I make enough to pay my bills and have a little fun."

"Sammy." I frowned. "That's not safe. Not in today's world."

"Not in any world. I know how my mom died, that's why I'm careful. I only work with guys I know."

"If you know it's not safe, why are you doing it? There are plenty of other jobs out there. You don't need to…"

"No job that pays what I make in an hour. I know what I'm doing. I'm not stupid. It's not like I do it that often." Sammy looked at her phone. "I should get going."

"Hey, do me a favor? Don't tell Cate you saw me, and I won't tell her I saw you." I stood up and gave her a hug. "You know you'll always be my baby sister?"

"I know." Sammy kissed my cheek. "Your secret is safe with me."

190

DEPENDING ON YOU

I took her hands in mine. "And you know if you need anything, you can call me. Any time of the day or night. I don't care what it is. If you need me, I'll be there. Take care of yourself, Sammy. Just because your mom did it, doesn't mean you have to. You have so much potential."

"I know, Mom." Sammy waved as she skipped away.

I was probably the last person Silas wanted to see after his time at the den of dysfunction, but I needed to find him. I walked over to his car to see if there was any way I could figure out how to find him. The idea of knocking on every door lost its appeal when I realized I may have to make small talk, or worse figure out who Sammy's client was.

"Can I help you?" The deep voice sent me into the air.

I placed my hand on my chest. "You scared the crap out of me."

"Patti?" Silas put his hands in his pockets. "What are you doing here? Why are you trying to break into my car?"

"I'm not. I wanted to see if I could tell what room you're staying in." I tightened the grip on my purse. "We need to talk."

Silas held up his phone. "You know how these things work, right?"

I hit my hand on my forehead. "Oh my god, I'm aging myself, aren't I?"

"You're a real nice lady and all, but I'm not interested in hooking up with anyone."

Laughter poured out of me. "That's what you think this is about?"

"Why else have you been acting so weird? And why are you snooping around my car at the hotel I'm staying at? How did you even know I was here?" He took a step back. "Were you following me?"

191

"No, I wasn't following you. I'm staying here, too. I had no idea you were here but when I saw your car, I wanted to find you. To talk." I held my hands up. "That's it."

Silas smirked. "Well, this is awkward."

"No, it's okay. I bet you have all kinds of girls hitting on you. It's an honest mistake."

"What do you want to talk about?" Silas unlocked his car. "Do you want to go get dinner with me? My treat, as long as you know it's not going to lead to anything."

"If it's not leading to dessert, I think I'll pass."

"Ah, good one." Silas chuckled. "Dessert sounds like a great idea. Get in, you can help me decide what I want to eat."

"You've been in Lawrenceville long enough to know there is no place to go around here. It's either pizza or whatever else they have at the pizza place."

"I was hoping there was some I hadn't discovered yet." Silas turned on the radio. "Even the music here is old."

"Watch it. This isn't old, it's from when I was a kid."

"Point proven." Silas snickered. "I'm joking, don't freak out on me."

"I'm sorry you had to witness all that earlier. I had no idea how upset Mr. Silver was going to get over meeting you. You're a good kid, I figured he'd make a couple snide comments and be done with it. He's not usually like that."

"I figured he'd be upset with me. I was more surprised by the drama between all the rest of you." Silas pulled into the parking lot. "What was that all about?"

"It's a long story." I unbuckled my seatbelt and looked out the window. "Cate and I used to come here all the time."

"You guys have been friends forever. I always wanted a friend like that."

DEPENDING ON YOU

"Not anymore. Cate won't talk to me. The first time since we met thirty-one years ago." I rested my head against the seat. "I deserve it. I hate me, too."

"Does it have something to do with what was going on earlier?" Silas asked.

I nodded. "It does. Everything seems to."

"Do you want to talk about it?" Silas pulled his keys out of the ignition.

"Not really." The smile crept up my face. "You're a nice boy. So thoughtful and kind."

"Well, I had great role models. I had everything I ever needed." Silas shifted in his seat. "I heard some good news."

"You did?" I turned to meet his gaze. "What about?"

"They found the files from the adoption agency." His smile spread. "I'm meeting with the PI tomorrow morning."

"They did?" I fought the scowl off my face, replacing it with a smile. "That is great news."

"I know. I want to tell Cate so she can stop her search, but it doesn't look like now is the best time." Silas put his hand on the door handle. "Are you ready to eat?"

I nodded. "Yeah, sure. Now that we've got something to celebrate."

Chapter Thirty-Five
PATTI

Sleep evaded me as my thoughts took over. The thumping of my heart pounding against my chest was the only sound I could focus on. The last twenty years disappeared, transporting me back to that night. The one where everything changed.

With no one to talk to I was taken deeper into the depths of despair. There was no way to crawl out of it this time. No distractions to pull me away long enough to forget. It was over. My life as I knew it was over. There was no way I could go back to my old life, or my new one. I gasped for air as the panic swallowed me.

I reached for my phone and stared at the blank screen. As my hand trembled, I dialed Silas's number. "Are you up?"

"I am now." Silas groaned. "What time is it?"

"I don't know. I can't sleep. Could you come over?" I closed my eyes as I waited for his response.

"Right now?" Silas cleared his throat. "It can't wait until morning?"

DEPENDING ON YOU

"No, it can't. I need to tell you something and I don't think I can make it to your room."

"Is everything alright?" Rustling on the other end of the phone made it hard to hear what he was saying.

"Silas, are you still there?" I sat up, placing my feet on the floor when I heard a knock on my door.

"Patti, let me in." Silas turned the doorknob. "Patti."

Silas was pressed up against my door when I opened it. "Hi." I bowed my head. "Come in. We need to talk."

Silas pulled out the desk chair and sat with his hands braced on his thighs. "What's going on?"

I sat on the bed and pulled the pillow close. "Silas, I don't know how else to say this, so I'm just going to say it." I took a deep breath. "I'm your birth mother. I'm the one who gave you away."

Silas nodded. "I know. Well, I assumed you were Patricia Thomas."

"You already knew?" I squeezed the pillow. "Why didn't you say anything earlier?"

"Because I didn't want to freak you out. And I had a feeling you would tell me when you were ready." Silas leaned back in his chair and crossed his arms.

"I didn't know what to do. I was young and terrified. It had nothing to do with you." My bottom lip quivered. "I'm so sorry."

"Don't be sorry, I'm not upset with you. It's thanks to you that I had such a great life." Silas scooted to the edge of the chair. "I don't know the circumstances of how you got hooked up with Trevor, but I'm guessing it's not a good story. He was so much older than you." I hid my face behind the pillow and sobbed. Silas sat next to me and put his hand on my back.

195

JESSICA AIKEN-HALL

"I didn't hook up with him. He raped me." My body trembled as fear danced with rage. "I didn't even know who he was."

"I'm so sorry, Patti. That must have been terrifying."

I blinked away the tears and nodded. "It was. I'd never been so afraid in my life."

"And you never told anyone about it, have you?" Silas rubbed my back. "Is that why you and Cate are fighting?"

"I never told anybody. I couldn't." I tightened my grip on the pillow.

"So, you've been holding onto this for the past twenty years? I can't imagine how hard that has been."

"I've never kept anything from Cate before. I didn't want to, but I didn't know what to do. I tried to tell her, but there was so much going on in her life. I didn't want to burden her with it. And then it was too late."

"Why was it too late? What happened?" Silas rested his elbows on his knees as he looked at me.

"I don't know." I held my head. "Everything got so complicated so fast. I got pregnant with Logan and married his father before I graduated college, and then it was too much to handle." I put my hand on his knee. "I felt so guilty every day I looked at my little boy when I didn't know where you were."

"It was a different circumstance. I understand." Silas put his hand on mine. "You don't have to keep beating yourself up over this. I don't blame you at all."

"But you should. I'm a terrible person. I don't deserve anything I have. My whole life has been a lie. Every day I pretended to be someone I wasn't. I don't even know who I am anymore."

"It's never too late to start over." Silas smiled. "Thank you

196

DEPENDING ON YOU

for telling me. It means a lot knowing you trusted me enough to tell me."

"I didn't really have a choice. I knew it was only a matter of time before you found out. I should have been on that website looking for you. I didn't even know about it. It's not because I didn't want to know how you were doing or where you were. It was because I didn't want to ruin anything for you."

"I'm glad we met." He yawned. "You're better than I could have imagined."

"How's that possible? I'm not worthy of your forgiveness." I pulled a tissue out of the box and blew my nose.

"You did what you thought was best for me. And you made the right choice. My parents love me and gave me everything I could have ever asked for. Not only did you do a good thing for me, but you helped them have a family."

"I should have done better."

"Patti, I don't think you could have. What were your options? If you kept me you would have been reminded of what happened to you every time you looked at me. Even if you didn't mean to, I'm sure I would have felt the resentment. Besides, you were just a kid when you had me."

"That's not an excuse." I rubbed the bridge of my nose. "There's more I haven't told you. Cate still doesn't know about you. This isn't why she's not talking to me."

Silas pulled his legs under him and turned to look at me. "Then what made her so upset?"

"You weren't the only secret I carried from that night." I took a long breath in before opening my eyes. "I'm the one how killed Trevor."

Silas squinted his eyes. "You killed him? How?"

"Does it really even matter?" I picked at my fingernail.

197

"It might help to get it out." Silas put his hands between his knees. "I'd like to know what happened."

"It was prom night and I wasn't ready for what my date had in mind, so we went to the ice cream shop where I worked and had our own little party there. It was the perfect end to a great night. The guy I went with was so sweet and understanding about my cold feet and he gave me the best kiss goodnight. He offered to take me home, but I told him I was fine to walk home. I needed to clean up the shop anyway. I'd walked home from there a million times before. Nothing ever happens in Lawrenceville."

I dug my fingernails into my hand as the memories cascaded over me. "I had just put my key in the door to lock it when he grabbed me." I put my hands to my neck. "This big man forced me into the building and pulled my dress up and..." I swallowed the bile rising in my throat. "Raped me. He ran off as soon as he was done with me. It's all a blur now, but I was so scared. The guy was long gone, but I stayed on the floor for a while until I felt safe enough to stand. When I got to my feet, I called Cate. I asked her to meet me at our place, the cemetery by the high school. Before I left the shop, I searched the place to find something to bring with me in case..." Shivers ran up my spine.

"The only thing I could find was a baseball bat the owner's kid left there after practice. I took it with me and ran to the cemetery as fast as I could. I didn't want anyone to see me." I covered my mouth. "I got to the top of the hill, where Cate was going to meet me, and the guy was behind me. I started swinging the bat and didn't stop until he fell to the ground. I ran away from him and waited for Cate. I never thought about her hitting him with the car. He was already dead. I just needed to get away from him. When Cate got there, she ran into his

DEPENDING ON YOU

body. She thought she had killed him. And I didn't tell her any different. I let my best friend take the blame for it all these years."

"Wait." Silas rubbed his hand over his face. "Cate took the blame, but you really killed him, and Detective Silver covered it up?"

"No, he didn't know anything about any of this until yesterday. Cate hit Trevor with her car, but he was already dead. I didn't tell her what I had done, because..." I sighed. "Well, it doesn't really matter. All that matters is that I killed him and let Cate think she did. I didn't own up to any of it and I ran away. I left her here to fend for herself. I made a new life and we slowly drifted apart."

"I don't understand why you wouldn't have told Cate what happened that night. You guys are best friends."

"It all happened so fast. I didn't know what to do. I wished I had done things differently, but at least now I can do the right thing. I'm going to turn myself in tomorrow."

"No, you're not." Silas shook his head. "There's no way I'm going to let you do that."

"I have to. I don't have a choice."

"There's no reason for you to do that. You're not a suspect. There's no evidence that you did anything." Silas shrugged. "As far as I'm concerned, you didn't do anything wrong."

"Silas, I did. I have to do this if I have any chance at fixing things with Cate."

He put his hand on my arm. "Please, don't do anything yet. Give me some time while I try to figure this out."

"Why do you want to help me?" I dried my eyes. "I'm not a good person."

"Because what I do know about you is that you're a great

199

JESSICA AIKEN-HALL

friend and an even better mother. You had every reason to kill Trevor. And if you didn't tell Cate then there had to be a good reason for that, too. I know you never meant to hurt anyone. I want to help you get your life back."

'I'm afraid it's too late for that. I appreciate how kind you're being to me and the offer, but this is something I need to do." I put my hand on his. 'I want to make you proud."

Chapter Thirty-Six

PATTI

I turned the TV on for some background noise while I sat alone in my room. Silas was already meeting with his PI, which seems pointless since he already knows everything. I hadn't heard from Katie or Logan in days. I remember being their age and being so caught up in my own life that nothing else mattered. I could only hope they wouldn't miss me when I have to leave them.

I wore down the carpet in front of the window as I paced the tiny space. Is this what jail is going to feel like? I chewed my fingernail as the unknowns filled the empty spaces. "What have I done?" My words echoed off the walls as I fell to the floor.

The ping of my phone caught my attention as my face was pressed against the musty carpet. I reached for it, hoping it was someone from home telling me how much they missed me, but it wasn't. A text from the eye doctor reminding me of an upcoming appointment for Katie. With the phone in my hand, I logged onto my Facebook account and found Jake's profile. It'd be good to see him before he hears on the news what I have

201

become. I sent the message and went back to my self-loathing party of one on the floor.

The quiet lull of the background noise was interrupted with a breaking news bulletin. I sat up to take notice. "Body of Trevor Martin, man from the cold case murder from 1998 has been ordered to be exhumed. We will cover the story as it unfolds."

I crawled to the bed and sprawled out. The window of opportunity to turn myself in before Cate has to get involved was shrinking before my eyes. Now that Silas knows the truth, he could turn on me, too. I wouldn't blame him.

I pounded my head into the mattress before rolling onto my back. The same thirty-four ceiling tiles greeted me as the room closed in around me. It was only a matter of time. That has been my moto since that night. It was only a matter of time before I got my period. Or before someone noticed I was pregnant. Or before someone found out. Or... the daunting list of possibilities seemed endless, until now. Time had run out.

The rap on the door made my heart stop. How could they know already? I scanned the room looking for a way out. But I was done running. I couldn't let Cate, or anyone else take the fall for this ever again. I swung my feet off the bed and walked to the door, taking a moment to compose myself. "Just a second."

When the door swung open a familiar face smiled back at me. "Patti?"

"Jake?" I ran my fingers through my hair. "How did you..."

Jake smirked. "I was in the area for work and saw your message. You said you were staying in town, so I went to the front desk and asked if you were here, and they gave me your room number." He shrugged. "The beauty of small-town living."

DEPENDING ON YOU

"Huh, well I guess some things never change." I held the door open and stepped out of the way. "Do you have time to come in?"

"I thought you'd never ask." He held his arms out. "Can I give you a hug?"

I rushed into his arms and couldn't hold the sadness in any longer. My body heaved under his strong arms.

He rubbed my back. "I missed you, too."

I lifted my head off his chest and tapped him. "Don't flatter yourself."

"Ah, there she is, there's the Patti I know." He tightened his grip around me before letting me go. "Is everything alright? How come you're not staying with Cate?"

I rubbed my eyes. "It's a long, messy story. I don't even know if she knows I'm still here."

Jake took my hand and led me to the bed, where we sat down. "I have time. Tell me what's going on."

I leaned my head back and closed my eyes. "I can't."

"You know you can tell me anything. I miss our talks." Jake smiled. "We had a lot of good ones."

My cheeks lifted. "We sure did."

"So, what's going on? Why are you in this shitty place all by yourself?"

"This wasn't part of the plan. I came back for Cate. Her dad's not doing well. He's on hospice. I was staying with them, until she kicked me out." My bottom lip quivered. "She told me I was dead to her."

Jake scrunched up his face. "Why would she say that? If you two aren't together there is something definitely screwed up with this world."

"You're right. There is something wrong, and it's me. Let's

203

just leave it at that." I lifted my shoulders. "I do have a favor to ask since you're here."

"You're going to leave me guessing what could have possibly caused the two of you to part ways and ask me to do something?" Jake rubbed his chin. "Sounds about right."

"Relax, you're going to like it." I nudged him in the side. "I need you to go see Cate, but you can't tell her I sent you."

Jake raised his brow. "Look, I want nothing more than to see Cate. I think about her all the time, but she made it very clear that she doesn't want anything to do with me. I don't have it in me to be rejected again."

"Please, Jake? It's important." I batted my eyes at him.

Jake groaned. "Don't do that. Don't make yourself so pathetic that I have to do what you ask me to."

"I need you to take her somewhere for me. It's going to sound strange, but trust me, okay?"

Jake dropped his head between his shoulders. "For the love of God, when will it end?"

"Oh, stop it, you know you want to. I know she'd love to see you. She told me before she vowed to never speak to me again."

"She was talking about me? Really?" Jake's body perked up. "Did you tell her I got divorced?"

"As a matter of fact, I did. She was pretty excited to hear the news. She needs a little nudge, that's all. I know when she sees you, all of her feelings will come back to her."

Jake chuckled. "Okay, well, since you put it that way, what do you need?"

"I need you to go to her place and tell her you need to show her something. Don't make it weird or she won't go."

Jake raised his brow. "How is there any way not to make that seem weird?"

DEPENDING ON YOU

"I don't know, use your dashing good looks and charm. You're a smart guy. Figure it out." I shook my head. "Once you get her to go with you, I need you to take her to my old house. When you get there, tell her you need her to take you to my treehouse."

Jake held his hand up. "Hold up. None of this sounds plausible. Excuse me Miss, I've been in love with you for the last two decades. Now come with me to the forest where we can frolic in your ex-best friend's treehouse. Which by the way isn't even your house anymore."

"Stop it. You're making it sound unreasonable." I put my hand on his arm. "I really need you to do this for me. I don't have anyone else to ask."

"Okay, I'll do it." Jake ran his hand through his hair. "Can it wait a day? If I'm going to see Cate, I want to look irresistible."

"It can wait a day, but not longer, okay?"

"There's no way I could let that carrot dangle over my nose for more than a day." Jake grinned. "So, what do I do once we get to your treehouse?"

"I need you to climb the ladder and go inside."

"Are you trying to get me killed?" Jake folded his arms and shook his head.

"Don't be a baby. If you fall you won't die. You might break your hip or something." I laughed. "When you're up there I need you to go to the back of the treehouse and find a tin box in the corner. I need you to bring it down and give it to Cate and tell her to open it."

"That's all, huh?" Jake shook his head. "If this is going to help the two of you fix whatever's going on, I'll do it."

"Thank you. I don't know how I'll repay you." I kissed his cheek. "You've always been my second best friend."

205

JESSICA AIKEN-HALL

"Well, there's a title to write home about." Jake laughed. "Are you sure you don't want to talk?"

"No, not yet anyway. Maybe we can be pen pals."

Jake twisted his face. "Pen pals? Why not just keep talking online like we have been?"

I shrugged. "I'm not sure I'm going to be able to be online much longer. Please don't hate me. You're all I have left."

Jake squinted. "I don't understand what's going on, but I could never hate you. No matter what."

"I hope so. I'd miss our friendship so much."

Jake stood up and stretched. "You know, the last time I was in this place was with Cate." He wiggled his eyebrows.

I walked him to the door. "Ask her what the treehouse was for. You'll get a chuckle out of it."

Chapter Thirty-Seven
CATE

"I need you to get Patti here." Dad lifted his head and coughed. "I need to talk to you girls."

"I'm not doing that. I never want to see her again." I folded my arms. "If you want to see her, ask Sammy to get her here but I don't want to be here when she is."

"Cate, that's enough. You girls have gone through too much to act like this. You didn't even give her a chance to explain herself." Dad grimaced. "I don't have much longer. I can feel it."

"Dad don't say that." I scowled. The anger kept the emotions at bay. "She had twenty years to explain. I don't owe her a damn thing."

"I'm not asking you, I'm demanding you bring her here." Dad poked his finger into the mattress. "I cannot take this to the grave."

"Then tell me. I'm here."

"I won't. I need both you girls and I'm only saying this once." Dad leaned his head into the pillows and closed his eyes. "Please, Catie Cat. I need you to do this for me."

I threw my hands up. "You've got to be kidding me. You really don't understand what she's done."

Dad raised his hand and waved it toward the door. "Now."

I stormed out of the living room to find Sammy. I banged on her locked door. "Hey, are you awake?"

"No, go away," Sammy grumbled.

"I need you to do me a favor." I leaned against the door and hit my hand on it. "I need you to go find Patti and bring her back here."

I stepped away from the door when I heard footsteps. Sammy poked her head out the door. "Why do you want me to do that?"

"Dad's demanding she comes back." I rolled my eyes. "Apparently, what I think doesn't matter."

"Okay, let me get dressed and I'll go get her." Sammy rubbed her eyes.

"How do you know where she is?" I raised my brow.

"She's at Hillside Inn, where else would she be?" Sammy closed the door in my face.

"How do you know she's still here?" I pressed my ear to the door.

"Because I saw her and I know she wouldn't just leave with Dad as sick as he is. She's not a monster."

"You obviously don't know her." I clenched my teeth.

Sammy pulled her T-shirt over her head as she walked out her door. "I don't know what happened between you, but you need to fix this. Patti is our sister. It's not up to you to throw her away."

"You have no idea what you're talking about. I don't even know who she is." I followed her outside. "Make sure you tell

DEPENDING ON YOU

her it's Dad who wants her here. I don't want her thinking this is my idea."

Sammy got into her car and waved. "We'll be back soon."

I went back inside and cleaned up the living room. The last thing I needed was for Patti to think I couldn't handle things. I stacked a pile of magazines and put them on the coffee table. After cleaning off the chairs I sat down and closed my eyes. I hadn't slept since Patti finally told me the truth.

SAMMY SHOOK ME AWAKE. "Hey, we're back. How's Dad doing?"

When I opened my eyes, I saw Patti huddled by the door. I pushed Sammy out of my way and stood up. "He's fine." I stretched my arms over my head and yawned. "I hope Sammy told you why you're here."

Patti nodded. "I understand."

Dad's lips turned up before he opened his eyes. "I'm so glad you're both here."

"How are you feeling?" Patti took a few steps closer to his bed.

"For God's sake, stop acting like we're strangers." He patted his hand on the bed. "Come have a seat."

Patti slinked past me. "I'm sorry." She dropped her head. "I don't want to make anyone upset."

"A little too late for that, don't you think?" I rolled my eyes.

"Sammy, would you mind going to the store and getting me some ginger ale?" Dad asked as he propped himself up.

"Okay." Sammy put her hands on her hips and looked at me. "Are you sure it can't wait?"

209

"No, I'd like it now." Dad shooed her to the door.

"What's this about Dad? Why did you need to have us both here?" I tapped my foot as I watched Patti get comfortable on Dad's bed.

"Come over here and find a place to sit." Dad held out his hand. "We need to talk." He looked up at Patti. "Remember when you asked me if there was anything I needed to get off my chest?"

Patti nodded. "I remember."

"Well, I'm ready to talk."

I sat on the other side of Dad and folded my arms. "What do you need to say?"

"I need you to know that what I'm going to tell you is going to be upsetting. I didn't ever want to have this talk, but I've run out of options." Dad took a long pause. "The night that sonofabitch died, I saw you girls leaving the cemetery. I was on patrol and happened to be in the right place at the right time."

"You knew it was us the whole time?" I asked.

"Give me a chance to finish before you ask questions, okay?" Dad coughed into his hand. "When I saw you girls leave the cemetery, I had this feeling in my gut that something was wrong. When I went to check it out, I found him on the ground. When I approached him, I knew who it was right away. I gave him a kick right to his side to see if the bastard was still alive. He rolled over to try to protect himself."

"He was still alive?" I looked at Patti before quickly looking away.

Dad held up his hand. "Please let me finish." He adjusted himself in the bed. "When Trevor called me by name, the anger raged straight through me. I didn't even think about it and pulled my gun out. One shot to the head was all it took." He

210

DEPENDING ON YOU

waved his hands. "The bane of my existence was finally gone. I spent the next few months covering my tracks so it looked like a drug crime. I knew a guy who knew a guy who helped change reports and I was hoping the whole thing would blow over."

"Why did you hate him so much?" I asked, not able to hold back my questions.

"He was the person your mother got the drugs from that killed her. She was staying with him, and my guess is he got sick of her and threw her out. I always thought he killed her, but I didn't have the evidence to charge him. The case was too personal for me to get involved and no one else gave a damn to do anything."

"He killed Mom?" My heart shot into my throat as memories from that night came. "Are you sure?"

"I'd bet my life on it." Dad snickered. "Although that doesn't really matter anymore. That guy was bad news. Killing him was the best thing that ever happened to this town."

"Mrs. Silver was dating him?" Patti lifted her head to ask.

"I'm not sure what they were doing. Guys like that don't really date, they just take what they want and move on." Dad rubbed his hand over his face. "This wasn't the first time they got tangled up together."

"What do you mean?" I scowled when I noticed the tears streaming down Patti's face.

"Trevor was Sammy's father." Dad closed his eyes and rested his head on his pillow. "I caught them together when I came home early from work. Your mother and I were having problems at the time. We hadn't slept together in months, and she rushes in with a positive pregnancy test. I knew the only chance of the baby having a normal life was to go along with it."

211

JESSICA AIKEN-HALL

Patti gasped and muttered something I couldn't understand.

"I knew you weren't Sammy's dad. I always knew it." I rolled my eyes. "And she goes around acting all..."

Dad shook his head. "Don't you ever tell her. There's no need in making her suffer. I'm her father. I'm all she ever knew."

I looked away as my cheeks burned. "I wouldn't do that."

"You have to promise me, no matter how upset you get with her, you'll never tell her." Dad placed his hand on mine. "Promise me."

"I promise."

"I needed you to know in case something was to happen to her. I know her lifestyle is much like your mother's, and I need you to be aware of anything that might be harmful to her."

"Dad, I can't promise to take care of Sammy for the rest of her life. I've tried. I don't have it in me any longer."

"I'll look after her." Patti cleared her throat. "Now that I'm not going to jail, I'll have plenty of time to help with Sammy."

"She's not your problem. We don't need your help." I crossed my arms. "Just because we finally know the truth, doesn't excuse all the lies. You're a stranger to me."

Patti nodded. "I understand, but if your dad wants someone to look after Sammy, I'll do it."

"What part of..."

"That's enough Cate." Dad raised his voice louder than I had heard him since before Mom died. "Thank you, Patti." He took her hand and rubbed his thumb over it. "I know you'll do a good job."

I rolled my eyes and sighed, turning away from them both.

"I'm not sorry I killed him, but I am sorry you girls let this ruin your lives. I had no idea you were both holding onto all of

212

this. I never would have let you suffer like this had I known. But please don't let it destroy your friendship." Dad's voice softened. "There's a lot to process. Give it some time, but don't walk away from what you two have. I know what doesn't make sense now will eventually."

Chapter Thirty-Eight
CATE

"Cate, someone is here to see you," Sammy yelled before going to her room.

I wiped my hands off on my jeans and went to the living room. My mouth dropped open when I saw him.

"Hi." Jake waved. "Your sister told me to come in." His smile awoke the butterflies in my stomach.

"What are you doing here?" I inched toward him.

He put his hands in his pockets and rocked on his heels. "I was in town and thought I'd stop by and say hi."

"Okay." I turned to look at Dad. He was still sleeping. I pushed Jake to the door.

"Wait, I can't leave, not yet."

"Let's go outside so we can talk." I put my hand on his back and guided him in the right direction.

"Oh, okay." Jake nodded as he went back outside. "It's nice to see you. It's been too long."

"It has." I pulled my eyes off him and looked at my feet. "I'm such a mess. I didn't expect anyone was going to see me like this."

DEPENDING ON YOU

"I think you look beautiful." He pushed his hair off his forehead.

"Thanks, but I know you're being nice." I folded my arms over my stained T-shirt. "So, how have you been?"

"Oh, you know. Busy doing nothing." Jake laughed. "How about you?"

"I've been here, taking care of my dad, trying not to kill my sister."

Jake looked down and kicked at the gravel. "I'm sorry to hear about your dad. That must be a lot to deal with."

"It is. I hate seeing him so sick. He's always been my hero." I sneered. "But I guess even heroes have their weaknesses."

"I don't think dying constitutes for a weakness." Jake rubbed the back of his head. "Um, this is going to sound weird, but do you want to go for a walk with me?"

"Why does that sound weird?" I looked behind me. "Let me make sure Sammy knows I'm leaving, and I'll be right back." I left him standing in the driveway and rushed to the bathroom. Looking in the mirror only fueled the anxiety. I put my hair into a ponytail and brushed my teeth before going to my room and finding a new shirt to wear.

I wiggled her doorknob. "Hey, Sammy, I'm going for a walk with Jake. Can you stay with Dad until I get back?"

She turned her music down and came to the door. "Are you going on a date?" She raised her brow and grinned. "If it means you might come back in a better mood, go have fun."

"Don't be gross. We're going for a walk." My face flushed.

"Whatever you old people call it, have fun. I'll hang out with Dad." She pushed me toward the front door. "Go, we'll be fine."

215

JESSICA AIKEN-HALL

Jake was waiting for me in the same place I left him. "So, where are we walking to?"

"You'll find out soon enough." Jake stuffed his hands in his pockets. "So, how have you been, besides stressed out and busy?"

"I honestly don't even know." I folded my arms and walked next to him.

"Why don't you know?" Jake stopped to look at me. "I shouldn't be here, right?" He hung his head and looked at the ground.

"No, that's not it at all. I'm glad to see you." I put my hand on his arm. "I've missed you."

"You have? Then how come you didn't call me or..."

"I don't have your number. And I didn't know you and Patti had kept in touch. Seems like there's a lot I don't know about her." I pulled my hand away and started walking.

"What do you mean? What happened between you two? I never thought I'd see the day that you two wouldn't be together."

"Me, either, but people change. They're not always who you think they are, even when you think you know every detail about them." I squeezed my eyes to fight back the tears.

"What did she do?" Jake asked.

"It's not really important." I shook my head. "How have you been?"

"Life has not been what I thought it would be. I got married to a woman I didn't love because I thought it was what I was supposed to do. Turning thirty does that, I guess. My dad kept telling me I was going to die alone, so when I started dating Vanessa, I asked her to marry me. I never loved her."

"How can you marry someone you don't love?"

216

DEPENDING ON YOU

Jake shrugged. "It's a long story, but it starts with you." He smiled. "It's hard to love someone when you gave your heart to someone else."

I fought back the urge to smile. "You love me?"

"I do. I never stopped. All that stuff they say about your first love is true." Jake covered his face. "You must think I'm pathetic."

I shook my head. "I never stopped loving you, either. I never dated anyone else. You were my first and my last."

Jake held his hand to his chest. "Really? Then why have we been living in our separate hells all this time when we could have been living the life we wanted?"

"That's a long story. Seems like there are a lot of those." The smile spread across my face. "I never imagined I'd be talking to you again."

"I knew we would. I knew if I wished hard enough, I'd get to see you again. There was no way I could have loved you as much and lived the rest of my life without at least another conversation."

"Is that all you want? A conversation?" I swallowed the hope I had been holding onto.

"No, that's not all I want, but it's a nice place to start." Jake held his hand out. "I love you Cate. I can die a happy man after today."

I laced my fingers with his. "I haven't walked down this way in years."

"Don't get upset with me, but there's a reason we went this way. And I'm going to need your help getting to where we're going." Jake squeezed my hand. "Please don't get mad at me."

"Why?" I squinted my eyes. "Where are we going?"

217

'I need you to bring me to Patti's tree house." He ran his fingers through his hair.

My feet became anchors not allowing me to move forward. 'I'm not going there."

Jake tugged at my hand. 'Aww, come on. I don't know why, but I feel like this is important."

'She put you up to this, didn't she? Is that the only reason you're here?" I pulled my hand out of his.

'No, that's not the only reason. It is why I came today, but I have been looking for an excuse to come see you the last two decades." Jake held his hand out. 'Please bring me to the treehouse."

'Why doesn't she bring you there?" I folded my arms. 'It's not even her property anymore."

'I know. That's why she said we should go this way." Jake held his forehead. 'I guess if you're not going to show me how to get there, I'll try to find it on my own."

I watched as he entered the path to Patti's treehouse. The deeper he went into the woods the more my curiosity grew. 'Jake, wait for me." I rushed through the overgrown grass and weeds.

'You didn't want to see me get mauled by a bear?" Jake laughed. 'I think I can see it."

'This place looks so much smaller." I took Jake's hand. 'It's this way."

At the base of the treehouse a flood of memories took my breath away. I felt like that seven-year-old hiding from all my problems. I covered my mouth as the emotions overtook me.

Jake put his arm around me and pulled me close. 'I shouldn't have made you come."

'No, it's okay. It's just that this place brings back so many

DEPENDING ON YOU

memories. Patti and I have been through so much together." I pushed the tears off my face and put my hand on the base of the tree.

"Patti asked me to ask you what the treehouse is for."

Laughter replaced the pain. "Oh my god. She did not."

"She did, and by the sounds of things I need to know." Jake smirked. "So, what's it for?"

"Patti made this into our love shack." I rolled my eyes. "We never used it for that, but for our last summer together she fixed this place up so we'd have a nice place for our first time."

"Oh, now I've got to take a look." Jake put his foot on the bottom rung. "Do you think this is going to hold me?"

"It should. It's only been sitting out here for the last thirty years. What could possibly go wrong?"

"That makes me feel so much better." Jake chuckled as he continued to climb up the ladder. "Do you get service out here if you need to call 911?"

I took my phone out to check. "If I hold it over here, I get one bar. That should be enough."

"Perfect." The top half of Jake disappeared into the tree-house. "This does not look like a love shack."

"I'm sure it doesn't. It's been a while since anybody's been up there." I stood at the bottom of the tree and tried to look up through the hole.

Jake slithered the rest of the way in. "I don't see it anywhere."

"What are you looking for?" I stood on the first step.

"I think I got it." Jake inched his body back to the opening.

"Got what? What are you talking about?" I stepped out the way as Jake came back down.

219

"I'm not sure what it is, but Patti wanted me to give this to you." He handed me a small tin box.

"Patti told you to give this to me?" I rubbed my hand over the top of the box. "Why?"

"I have no idea. She said it was important that you got it." He wiped his hands off on his pants. "Well, go ahead and open it."

I pried the lid off the box and pulled out folded up paper. "It looks like a letter."

"What's it say?" Jake put his hands on his hips.

I handed the tin to Jake and unfolded the yellowed paper. "*Dear Cate.*" I looked over at Jake. "What is this?"

He shrugged. "I have no idea. Read it and find out."

I cleared my throat. "*I'm writing this letter because I have some things I need to tell you, but I don't know how. I have never kept anything from you for as long as we've known each other and it's killing me that I have to.*" I flipped the paper over to look for a date. "When did she write this?"

"I don't know, keep reading and you might find out."

"*The reason I called you to the cemetery that night was because I needed to tell you something. After Andrew and I left you and Jake we went to the ice cream shop and talked. I stayed behind to clean up the shop after Andrew left. When I went to lock the door, a man was waiting for me. I didn't see him until it was too late. He raped me.*" I covered my mouth. "Oh my god. That's why she was so upset that night."

"Wow, I don't even know what to say." Jake put his hand on my back. "Is there more?"

I nodded. "*After I called you, I went right to our spot to wait for you, but the guy must have followed me. I wasn't thinking and I killed him. When you arrived, he was already dead. I was so scared. I didn't know what to do. And I knew you'd be finding out about your mom in the morning. I didn't want you to have to take care of me when you would need me. A few weeks later, I found out I was pregnant. I couldn't tell you or anyone. I had a beautiful baby boy that I gave up for adoption.*" I covered my mouth. "Oh my god. Silas is her son."

"Who's Silas?" Jake's hand was still on my back.

"The kid who came to town looking for his birth father's killer."

"I've really been gone too long." Jake sighed. "She killed someone? And you've known about it all these years?"

I shook my head. "There's more to it than that."

"More to it? How can there be?" Jake looked over my shoulder. "Is there more?"

I nodded. *Every time I've tried to tell you, something has gotten in the way. It's killing me to keep this from you, but I don't know how to fix it. I can only hope you will find this letter and know how much I love you. I want to make this right, I just don't know how. Love you forever, Patti.*" My body trembled as I folded the letter back up. "I can't believe she never told me."

"I can't believe she never told anyone. That's a lot to have to carry all on your own."

"I know." I pushed the tears off my cheeks. "I need to find her."

"I can bring you to the Hillside Inn if you want." Jake rubbed my back before pulling me into his arms. "I think she'd love to hear from you."

"I don't know. I was so mean to her." I pressed my face into Jake's chest and sobbed. "I'm such an awful person."

"No, you're not." The safety of his arms brought me back

to prom night. When life was as good as it was ever going to be, before it all went wrong.

"If she wasn't trying to protect me none of this ever would have happened." I took Jake's hand. "Will you take me to her?"

"Absolutely. I'd love nothing more than for the two of you to get back together. It's like the reunion of my favorite band, except it will suck a lot less."

"Not everything is meant to last forever." I pushed my cheeks. "But some things are."

Chapter Thirty-Nine

PATTI

The banging on the door made me jump out of my skin. I closed my eyes and took a deep breath. Everything I had been afraid of all these years now seemed so insignificant, but the fear still lingered. "Who is it?" My hand hovered above the doorknob.

"It's Silas, let me in. I need to tell you..." He fell into the room when I opened the door. "Something." He caught his breath as I ushered him in to my room.

"What's wrong?" I studied him, trying to see what pieces of me he carried.

"You didn't kill Trevor. It wasn't you." Silas paced the room. "He was shot."

"I know." I folded my arms, trying to decide how much of the secret was mine to share.

"What do you mean you know? You told me you hit him with a bat. And if that's true, you're not responsible for his murder. Patti, that means you don't have to turn yourself in." Silas smiled. "It means I didn't mess everything up."

223

"You didn't mess anything up." I put my hand on his back and led him to the bed. "Sit with me for a minute."

"Why do you look upset? This is good news. You're not in trouble." Silas leaned forward on his knees.

"I have a lot on my mind." I rubbed my forehead. "If I tell you who shot Trevor, can we keep it between us? At least for now?"

"You know who shot him?" Silas narrowed his eyes. "Was it you?"

"No, I wish it was, though." I rolled my neck between my shoulders. "Do you promise me you won't tell anyone what I'm about to tell you?"

"Of course." Silas sat up and arched his back.

"Mr. Silver shot Trevor after Cate and I left. I still can't believe it. The last twenty years Cate and I both thought we killed him."

"Detective Silver shot him?" Silas rubbed his hand over his face. "No wonder he was so mad about me sticking my nose where it didn't belong. But why did he do it?"

"That's his story to tell, but let's just say the two of them had a history." I put my hand on his back. "And it looks like you have another half-sister."

"Another one? Did you..."

"No, not me." I put my hands on my legs and looked at Silas. "Trevor did. And you'll never guess who it is."

"I have no idea." Silas rubbed his eyes. "This is way more than I could have ever imagined."

"You and me both." I laughed. "The good news is you've already met your half-sister and the weird part is I always thought of her as my little sister."

"Cate?" Silas squinted his eyes. "How is that possible? He wasn't that much older than her."

"It's not Cate, it's Sammy." I held my hands out at my sides. "That's part of the reason Mr. Silver hated Trevor. Isn't small town living grand?"

"This is such an intertwined web of lies. I can't even wrap my head around it. It's too much." Silas held his head.

"Tell me about it." I laughed. "We always said we were family. It was truer than any of us realized."

"What are we going to do with this information? We can't pretend we don't know." Silas stood up and put his hands on his hips. "Detective Silver has to tell the truth. It's the only way to put this all behind you."

"No, I don't want him bothered about this. He's very sick. The last thing I want is for him to be interrogated. We will deal with whatever happens, but he needs to die in peace."

"But that means you might not be able to live in peace. Doesn't that bother you? He'll be long gone, and this may get pinned on you." Silas scratched his head. "I don't want you to go to jail."

"Silas, you promised me. We cannot tell anyone about this. We will deal with it when the time comes."

"Look, I didn't know what I was promising. That's not fair. I don't want to lose you." Silas looked away. "Don't you want to get to know me?"

"Of course, I do. We have so much lost time to catch up on, but I can't let Mr. Silver down, not when he needs me the most." I put my hand on his back. "I'll figure this out."

"Why do you care? Cate's not even talking to you. What does it matter?" Silas threw his hands up. "Why not expose the truth once and for all?"

JESSICA AIKEN-HALL

"Because I love Mr. Silver and Cate. We've been through too much for me to turn my back on them now. Besides, it might not even matter. They may figure it out on their own. I can only hope it's after Mr. Silver is gone."

"I don't understand why you're so loyal when he let you take the fall for this for so long. Doesn't that make you angry?" Silas crossed his arms. "Because I'm furious and I just met you."

"I'm not angry. I'm grateful. I know it sounds strange, but if Mr. Silver didn't finish the job I started, Trevor would still be alive. If he had survived, I would have been living in fear. What Mr. Silver did was protect me and all the rest of the girls in this town if he knew it or not."

Silas sighed. "You're way too nice. I don't think I'd be able to look at it the way you do. I guess I've never had anyone that important in my life."

"Well, stick around with me and you will." I put my arm around his waist and pulled him close. "The whole part of living is finding people worth risking it all for."

"So, there's no way of talking you out of this, huh?" Silas smiled. "And you're right, they may never even know you were there. If we can keep it that way there shouldn't be anything to worry about."

"That's right. Let's not worry about problems that might not happen."

"I wished I would have met you before I stirred this case up. If I'd had known what I know now I wouldn't have wanted to get Trevor justice. He's the last person who deserves any resources used on him. Detective Silver was right, we're all better off without him in our lives." Silas hung his head.

"How would you have known? It's not like anyone could have ever imagined it was all going to turn out this way. I'm just

226

DEPENDING ON YOU

glad I got to meet you and that you aren't a thing like that monster."

"I told my mom about you. She would like to meet you sometime." Silas smiled. "She was worried about what I might find. She had no idea."

We laughed before embracing in a hug. "She sounds like a lovely lady. I'd love to meet her. I have a few loose ends I need to tie up back home but once I get that taken care of I should have time for a visit. Unless I get arrested." I shrugged. "Then she'll have to come visit me."

"I have to get back home. Is it okay to call you?" Silas put his hands in his pocket. "I understand if you're not ready to have me in your life yet."

"I'm ready." I smiled. "You can call me anytime you want."

"But what about your husband and kids? Won't it upset them to know about me?" Silas lifted his shoulders.

"That's not for you to worry about. I'm not ashamed of you. You're no longer my secret. I'm not that scared teenager. I'm ready to do the right thing." I took his hands in mine. "I know we just met, but I love you and I want to be there for you from now on."

"Thanks, Patti. That means a lot." Silas nodded. "It's going to be cool to have two moms."

"Let me know when you get home. I'll be worrying until I hear from you." I kissed his cheek.

"Maybe having two moms isn't that great of an idea after all." Silas laughed. "I'm just kidding. I know it's going to be great." Silas gave me a hug before he shut the door behind him.

Being his mom was something I needed to do right. Thankfully the parents who raised him were kind people. He had a good life. Now it's time to make sure he has the best rest of his

JESSICA AIKEN-HALL

life that he can. Katie and Logan will be surprised at first, but they're good kids. I know they'll come around. As I watched him get into his car and drive away my heart fluttered in my chest. The pain of letting him go all those years ago was finally releasing its hold over me.

Chapter Forty

CATE

"Are you sure this is the right room?" I looked back at Jake and continued to knock on door.

"Yeah, she was here the other day." Jake pressed his face against the window. "The room looks empty. Do you think she could have gone home?"

"It's empty?" My shoulders fell with disappointment. "She must have. I thought she would have at least tried to stop by again."

"By the sounds of things, you weren't very nice to her. I probably would have left, too. She does have kids to get back to." Jake rubbed his chin. "Let me send her a message."

"Why didn't you think of that before?" I chewed at my fingernail as I waited for him to send the message.

"I didn't think about it. I figured she'd be here." He stared at his phone. "She's not online. If she's driving, I'm not sure when she'll get it."

"She doesn't have her car here. How could she be driving?" I folded my arms and sighed. "Come on, let's get out of here."

"She could have gotten a rental, or maybe her husband

229

came and got her." Jake pulled himself away from the window. "I thought she would have at least waited for me to get back."

"What's her hurry?" I scanned the parking lot as we walked to Jake's car. "You don't think she went to the police, do you?"

"Why would she go to the police? To turn herself in?" Jake opened the car door for me.

"No, there's a lot more to the story. I need to get home to my dad." I buckled my seatbelt and held my forehead. "I shouldn't have been such a jerk."

"Hey, I don't know what's going on, but I do know how much Patti loves you. She wouldn't do anything to hurt you." Jake put his arm behind my head as he backed out of the parking spot. "After I drop you off, I can try to find her if you want."

"I don't know." I rubbed the bridge of my nose. "There's so much going on right now. I'm not sure what to focus on."

Jake reached his hand over. "You're not in this alone. Let me help. I have some time I can take off work and help. I can do whatever you need."

I put my hand in his and felt my body relax. "You don't have to do that."

"I know. I want to. We've been apart for too long. Give me the opportunity to make up for lost time."

"Thank you." I closed my eyes and let myself soak up the moment with Jake. "I'm so glad Patti made you come see me."

Jake smiled. "See, if she was planning on doing anything bad, she wouldn't have done that. She loves you Cate."

"I know." I squeezed his hand. "I just don't like being apart from her. I don't feel complete without her."

"But you are. You two complement each other, but you don't need her to be complete. You're amazing all on your

DEPENDING ON YOU

own, just like she is. It's dangerous to depend on someone so much."

"Sounds like you're speaking from experience," I said.

"Yeah. It took me a couple times before I figured it out, but the sooner I realized I had everything I needed inside of myself, the better off I was. The hardest loss was my mom, but you were a close second." Jake bit his bottom lip.

"I'm sorry I hurt you. I was trying to protect you."

"From what?" Jake glanced over at me.

I rested my head against the seat. "It's a story for another day. Let's just say nothing was what I thought it was. The last twenty years of my life have been an illusion."

"I'll listen anytime you're ready to talk." Jake pulled in behind a black Dodge Charger.

I unbuckled my seatbelt and looked over at Jake. "Silas is here." My heart shot into my throat when the reasons behind his visit raced through my mind. "Patti must have told him."

"Told him what?" Jake chased after me. "Cate, what's going on?"

I rushed into the house. Jake trailed behind me. Silas had a chair pulled up next to the bed. "What are you doing here?"

Dad held his hand up. "Cate, everything is fine."

"Why is he here? Where's Patti?" I approached the bed and crossed my arms. "Dad, don't tell him anything."

"Cate, relax. We're having a nice conversation. Come sit down." He patted the side of his bed.

I sat, putting myself between them. "Why are you here? Did Patti send you?"

Silas shook his head. "No, she actually told me not to come, but I couldn't go home without at least talking with Detective Silver."

231

"Then why are you here?" I narrowed my eyes. "He's a sick man. He doesn't have time for any of this."

"I know." Silas cleared his throat. "But Patti could go to jail for something she didn't do. And I know neither one of you would want that to happen."

"He's right, Catie. I need to do the right thing. It's not fair for me to die holding onto this. What will it matter after I'm dead? I'd kill the sonofabitch again if I had the chance." Dad smirked. "I know I'm not supposed to say stuff like that, but I can't help it."

Jake stood by the front door with his hands in his pockets, turning his back to us and shifting weight from foot to foot.

"Dad, you don't have to do this. You even said there was no evidence at the scene. There's no way to pin this on either one of us."

"No, I don't want to leave this Earth without cleaning up this mess. It's the least I can do." Dad put his hand on my arm. "The police are on their way."

"Dad, no, please let's talk this through first." I stood up and looked out the window, brushing past Jake.

"Cate, if it's what he wants to do..." Jake reached for my arm.

I brushed Jake off me. "You don't understand. I don't want everyone to remember him like this. He was the best detective in this town. This isn't the legacy he should be leaving behind."

"Cate, why does it matter? If that's how people choose to remember me, that's their problem. If this one thing tarnishes my reputation, so be it. I don't want even a chance that either one of you girls will take the fall for this." Dad coughed. "This is important to me."

My shoulders fell when I saw the police car pull into the driveway. "This isn't how it's supposed to be."

Jake placed his hand on my back. "It will be okay." He put his arm around me and pulled me close. "It's important for you to let him do this."

"I know this will mean a lot to Patti. You're doing the right thing, sir." Silas stood up and put his hands in his pockets. "Thank you, Detective." He bowed his head as he walked out the door.

"There's still time to change your mind." My bottom lip quivered. "Please think about what you're doing."

Jake took my hand. "It's okay, Cate. This is what he wants to do."

"I can't..." I covered my mouth and bit down on my hand.

The knock on the open door brought my attention in the direction of the officer standing in front of us. He took off his hat and lowered his head. "I'm here to see Norman Silver."

Jake cocked his head and took a step back. "No way."

A smile spread across the officer's face. "Jake?" He reached his hand out to shake Jake's hand. "It's been forever man." He nodded at me. "You and Cate got back together?"

Jake's cheeks reddened as he put his hand behind his head. "We're getting reacquainted."

"Nice to see you Cate." Dimples accentuated his face.

"Andrew? I didn't know you were a cop." I folded my arms and studied the man in front of me. "I haven't seen you in ages."

"I'm a special agent." He elbowed Jake in the ribs. "I was just promoted. I work for the state. I haven't been in Lawrenceville since my father's funeral."

"I'm sorry, I had no idea. Life just kind of slipped by. I don't even know where it went." Jake hung his head.

"Aw, no worries. I know how it is." Andrew pulled out his note pad. "So, have you seen Patti?"

I looked to Jake and waited for him to answer.

"I saw her the other day. We were actually looking for her this afternoon. She probably went back home." Jake shrugged.

"I don't want to interrupt, but if you want to talk to me before I croak, you better get over here." Dad lifted his head and coughed.

Andrew gave us a small wave and walked over to Dad. "Sorry about that, sir." He bowed his head. "Is it okay if I have a seat?"

"It's fine with me." Dad fiddled with the controls on his bed.

"Do you want some help getting more comfortable?" I took the remote and helped him get in a more upright position. I put a pillow under his arm and got him as straight as he could sit. "Is that okay?"

"I'm fine." Dad shooed me away. "Go take your friend outside."

"I want to stay in here with you." I crossed my arms and stood my ground.

"I need to do this on my own. Everything will be fine. Don't worry about me." Dad forced a smile and waved. "Go on."

Jake held his hand out. "Come on, let's go see if Patti answered me yet."

I turned my head and watched Dad and Andrew as long as I could before I got to the door. "Andrew, be good to him. Please."

234

DEPENDING ON YOU

Andrew nodded. "Of course. We're just going to talk about some things."

Jake pulled my hand until we were both outside. "You've got to trust your dad. He needs to do this."

I bit at my fingernail. "You must be wondering what that was all about, huh?"

"I think I got the gist of it." Jake ran his hand through this hair. "So, this must be what Patti was talking about the other day."

"She told you?" I put my hand to my neck. "And she told Silas. Who else did she tell?"

"She didn't tell me anything. She told me we could be pen pals and asked me not to hate her when I found out." He rubbed his hand over his face. "So, she knows? That your dad..."

"Yeah, he told us both. I guess it's easier to die knowing you don't have any secrets. But I can't believe she told Silas. Why would she do that?" I put my hands on my hips. "Oh my god, she must have told him." I covered my mouth.

"That must be why he talked to your dad. He knows she's his mother." Jake leaned his head back. "Wow, this is unbelievable, it just keeps coming."

"Oh, there's more." I crossed my arms and blew out my frustration.

"More? How could there be?" Jake sat on the hood of his car.

"Silas has a sister." I looked around to make sure we were alone.

"Wait, Patti had another baby?" Jake scrunched up his face.

"No, it's way better than that." I kicked at the loose gravel. "Sammy's his sister."

235

JESSICA AIKEN-HALL

Jake cocked his head. "Sammy, as in your little sister?"

"Yup, it's crazy isn't it?" I raised my brow. "Now see why I didn't want to involve you in my real-life soap opera?"

"It wouldn't have scared me away. I would have been by your side through all of it." Jake rested his elbows on his knees.

"I didn't want to burden anyone with this mess. And to be honest, I thought I killed the guy, so learning the truth is news to me, too." I threw my hands up. "I'm not sure how much more I can take. My whole life has been a lie."

"Not your whole life. There's been some truths in there." He smiled. "Like prom night. That was as true as it gets."

"It was a nice night. Probably one of the best ones of my life." I stood in front of him and put my hands on his knees. "I'm sorry if I didn't make you feel special."

"Do not apologize. Even before all of this it sounds like there was a lot going on for you. I get why you pushed me away, but you don't have to. I want to walk through this life with you." Jake put his hands on top of mine.

"Do you think they're going to make my dad go to jail? Can they do that?"

"I'm not sure how it works. I'd hope they wouldn't do that. We'll have to wait and see. We'll figure it out, no matter what happens." Jake got off the car and hugged me. "Can I kiss you?"

I leaned into him and let my lips melt into his. "I missed this."

"Me, too." He pulled me closer and held my face. "You're so beautiful."

Looking into his eyes I could see the sincerity. It was like we picked up where we left off all those years ago.

236

Chapter Forty-One

PATTI

After spending time in my old treehouse, I knew it was time to find Cate. I couldn't leave town without at least trying to mend things between us. I took the shortcut through the woods so the new owners of the house wouldn't see me. I wasn't sure who they were, but it was likely they wouldn't want me walking around their property. The last thing I needed was for them to call the police on me.

When I turned onto the road to Cate's house, I saw the line of cars on the driveway. I covered my eyes with my hand to block the glare. I picked up my pace, hoping I wasn't too late to say goodbye to Mr. Silver. When I got closer to the house, I noticed the police cruiser in the driveway. "Oh my god, no." I covered my mouth as my heart raced.

When I caught my breath, I walked as fast as I could. I wasn't sure what I could do, but I had to at least try. An embracing couple stood in front of the cars. I squinted my eyes. "Cate? Jake?"

Cate broke out of his arms and wiped her mouth off. "Patti,

237

I'm so glad to see you." She rushed over to me and wrapped her arms around me. 'I thought you went back home."

'You're happy to see me?" My body trembled in her arms. 'Does this mean you don't hate me anymore?"

'I could never hate you. I'm sorry for all the awful things I said to you." Cate squeezed me tighter. 'I love you, Patti. Jake showed me your letter. I'm so sorry..."

'I'm sorry. I never wanted to keep any of it from you. I got in over my head and I didn't know what to do." I pulled out of her arms. 'I wrote that letter after I gave Silas up for adoption. I was hoping you'd find it. I wanted you to know."

'I wished I had gone back to the treehouse. After everything happened, I stopped doing anything that might have brought me joy. I didn't think I deserved to be happy," Cate said.

'I know, I failed you. I was too caught up in my own stuff to even notice how it was affecting you. Can you forgive me?" I blinked away the tears.

'You're forgiven. I don't want to waste any more time. We can't get back the years we lost, but we can make up for lost time now."

'You don't know how happy that makes me." My bottom lip quivered as I tried to fight off the emotion waiting to spill out. 'What's going on inside?"

Cate sighed and looked at Jake. 'Silas came by and convinced Dad to confess."

I covered my mouth and closed my eyes. 'Please tell me that's not what's happening."

'I wish I could." Cate shrugged. "They've been in there for a while."

'What's going to happen? Are they going to arrest him?

DEPENDING ON YOU

Can we make bail, or whatever?" I asked trying to find a solution to the problems brewing inside.

"All we can do is be patient and wait to see what happens." Jake put his hand on my back. "I'm so glad you two are back together."

"You and me both." I sniffled. "Should we go inside and see what's going on?"

Jake smirked at Cate. "No, I think it's best if we stay out of the way like Mr. Silver asked."

"We can't let them take him. I'll tell them he's covering for me," I said.

"But that's not true. We all know that now. And it seems like it's something Dad needs to do." Cate put her arm around me.

Cate spun me around when we heard the front door open and pushed me forward.

"Patti?" The voice pulled me back to simpler times.

"Andrew?" My mouth dropped open.

He took his hat off and stood in front of me. "You look great."

I folded my arms to cover the extra weight. "So do you."

He held his arms out. "Is it okay if I give you a hug?"

I nodded and took a step closer to him. "What are you doing here?"

"I was assigned to the cold case that was reopened and was told Detective Silver needed to talk to me." Andrew gave me a squeeze before letting me go.

"And?" I looked into his deep brown eyes. "What's going to happen?"

Andrew put his hat back on and grinned. "The case has been closed. Mystery solved."

239

"What happens to Mr. Silver?" I swallowed the lump creeping up my throat.

"Nothing. Seems like there was a misunderstanding. Detective Silver did a stellar job putting the pieces together. I just needed to connect the dots. The victim was involved in drug trafficking. It appears he was murdered by an unhappy dealer. Case closed." Andrew winked. "It was so nice to see you all."

"So, that's it? The case is closed now?" Cate stood by my side.

"Yup, I'm headed back to the barracks to write the final report and expedite this. Seems like we've wasted enough resources on this one." Andrew shook Jake's hand. "Are you going to be around town for awhile? I'd love to get a beer and catch up."

"That sounds great." Jake walked him to his cruiser where they finished their conversation.

Cate and I went into the house, where Mr. Silver was in bed. "Patti, it's so nice to see you." He reached out his hand. "I wasn't sure we'd get this chance."

"What happened?" Cate sat on the edge of his bed.

Mr. Silver's face lit up. "I said my peace. Special agent Weston wrote it all down and told me the case was closed."

"You told him everything?" Cate asked.

"Every detail. He agreed the sonofabitch had it coming. No need in beating a dead horse." Mr. Silver laughed.

"Did you tell him everything?" My cheeks burned at the thought.

"I told him what he needed to know." Mr. Silver patted the bed next to Cate. "Sit."

I squeezed in next to Cate and Mr. Silver. "Neither one of

you have anything to worry about. Let go of that night and move forward."

Cate and I looked at each other and nodded in agreement.

"I love you girls. You'll be okay. I know it in my heart." He put his hand to his chest. "I'm going to take a nap while you two catch up. I'm tired." He closed his eyes.

Chapter Forty-Two
CATE

The crowd filled the church and overflowed onto the front lawn as most of the town came to pay their respects to Dad. Patti, Sammy and Jake sat next to me in the front row as the minister told stories of the man I looked up to my whole life. "He was an honorable man who loved this town and his family even more. If you knew Detective Silver your life is better for it."

I wiped a tear off my cheek as I looked at Dad peacefully resting in his casket. He was able to protect all of us and still die a hero in the eyes of so many. His years of hard work and determination spoke volumes to his character. Everything he did, he did for a reason. Good or bad, there was always justification for the action.

"Do you think Mom is with him?" Sammy blew her nose.

I paused to find the right words. "I can only hope the woman Dad loved is by his side. He deserves only the best."

"I hope so. I don't want to think about him being alone." Sammy put her head on my shoulder.

DEPENDING ON YOU

'He's not alone. I'm sure he's already solving crimes wherever he is." Patti put her hand on Sammy's knee.

'Or committing them." I covered my mouth to hide the laughter. 'I'm sure Patti's right. He's in a better place doing all of the things he loves."

'He's the lucky one." Sammy blew a kiss to Dad. 'Do you think he'll miss us?"

'I don't think he'll have to." I pushed Sammy's hair out of her face. 'He'll check in on us and make sure we're doing okay."

'You think he's going to know everything we do? Like everything?" Sammy dabbed at her eyes.

Patti nodded. 'I do, Sammy. We have to make sure we do our best."

Sammy dropped her head and sobbed.

'What's that about?" I whispered.

Patti held her finger to her lips then mouthed the words, 'I'll tell you later."

After the church emptied, Jake drove us to the cemetery while we waited for Dad to arrive. 'Why isn't Dad being buried with Mom?" Sammy asked.

'I think he'd want it that way. Besides, this cemetery is such a beautiful place." I put my hand on Sammy's knee. 'He's going to have a room with a view."

Patti laughed. 'I don't know if you can call it a room."

'You know what I mean." I poked her with my elbow. 'Thank you for being here with me."

'I wouldn't miss this for anything. We're family." Patti winked.

'True." I smiled. 'Funny how things work out, isn't it?"

'It sure is." Patti took Sammy's hand and got out of the car. 'Come on, let's give your dad the sendoff he deserves."

243

JESSICA AIKEN-HALL

Jake put his arm around me. "How are you holding up?"

"I'm doing okay. Better than expected. I know he's free. In every way. What more could I ask for?"

"That's a great way to look at it." Jake gave me a squeeze. "He sure did a good job with you."

"I couldn't have asked for a better dad." I put my arm around his waist.

"The very place that stole everything from all is the one that brought us together." Patti ushered Sammy in our direction.

Sammy pulled her hands into her sleeves. "I think I want to go to rehab. I don't want Dad to see me like this."

Patti pushed Sammy's hair out of her face. "That's the best gift you can give him and yourself. You have a bright future ahead of you."

"I'm proud of you, Sammy. I'll do whatever you need." I reached for her hand. "We're stronger together. Always."

"I'm only a phone call away and I can be back in eight hours. Six on a good day." Patti smirked. "I can help you find a great place. There are a few down by me. You could stay with me until you get in, if you want. It might be good to get away from the friends keeping you stuck."

"I can go home with you?" Sammy dried her eyes. "You'd let me do that?"

"Of course. As long as it's okay with Cate." Patti's eyes glistened as she looked at me.

"If it's good for Sammy, it's fine by me." I tugged at Jake's shirt and smiled. "I think I'll be in good company."

Jake cleared his throat. "Sounds like a great plan, Sammy."

As they lowered Dad's body into the ground everything began to make sense. The pieces of me that had always felt like

244

they were missing were now whole. I was complete on my own. Having Patti, Sammy and Jake only made it better. Sometimes the greatest tragedies are followed by the greatest joy.

Chapter Forty-Three

PATTI

The long drive home gave me plenty of time to think. I knew exactly what I needed to do and for the first time in my life I was going to do what was best for me. With one more deep breath I looked at myself in the rearview mirror. The reflection looking back at me was one I had lost so long ago. "You can do this."

My heart shot into my throat when I saw Danny getting into his car. "Where are you going?"

"Why does it matter to you?" He rolled his eyes as he sank into the bucket seat. "What, now you suddenly care where I go?"

"I've always cared. I just never had the nerve to say anything." My fingernails dug into my palm as I gripped my purse strap.

"Oh, so now you're a changed woman? Why don't you go scrub the toilet and make some dinner? Then we can talk." Danny reached for the door.

I took a step forward, blocking him from shutting me out. "We need to talk."

246

DEPENDING ON YOU

"I don't have time for this. I'm running late." Danny put his hands up. "You've been gone too long to come here and tell me what to do. We can talk when I get home."

I shook my head. "No, this can't wait. I have some things I need to tell you." I looked in the backseat. "Your golf buddies will understand."

"I don't know who you think you are, but the kids and I have been fine without you. It's not earth shattering that you're back. The world doesn't revolve around you." Danny pushed me out of the way.

"Don't touch me." I stayed firmly planted in place. "Either you get out of this car or I'll make a scene. I'm sure one of the neighborhood kids will love to put it online. We can be the next viral video. Then everyone will be able to see who you really are."

Danny crossed his arms. "What is so important that you have to be such a..."

"Such a what?" I folded my arms tight against my chest. "Go on, say it."

Danny's tone softened. "Don't be so difficult. Let me go play with the guys and we can talk when I get home."

"I want a divorce. I can't live like this anymore. We don't have anything in common. God knows how many people you've been screwing." My shoulders fell. "Go have fun."

"Sounds like you've made up your mind." Danny rubbed his chin. "You can tell the kids."

"I plan on it. Oh, and by the way, I met the son I put up for adoption when I was eighteen. The kids will be meeting him, too." I pushed the hair off my shoulder and walked away.

"I always knew you were a whore." Danny slammed his door and maneuvered his car past the rental parked behind him.

247

JESSICA AIKEN-HALL

When I opened the front door, I was greeted by the explosion of a mess. Dirty dishes spilled out of the sink, empty food boxes covered the counters, and my feet stuck to the floor. "Katie! Logan!" I yelled over the thumping sound of bass pouring down the hall. "I'm home."

I set my bags down and knocked on their doors. "Guys, can you come to the living room?" I sat on the couch and waited for them.

"Hi Mom." Katie fell onto the sofa next to me. "How was your trip?"

"It was exhausting, but it was nice catching up with Cate." I let her hair fall through my fingers. How did you hold up without me?"

"We managed to survive. Barely." She laughed. "I missed you."

"I missed you and your brother, too."

"Not Dad, huh?" She rolled over to look at me.

"Not so much, that's sort of what I want to talk to you guys about."

"He was gone the whole time you were. He told us to keep our mouths shut, but I don't want to do that. It's not fair that he gets to be such a jerk and we're supposed to do what he says." Katie sat up. "I didn't want to hurt your feelings, but it looks like you're sick of him, too."

"I'm sorry you and Logan had to fend for yourselves. I didn't know you were on your own." I folded my hands and rested them in my lap. "And I'm sorry your father wasn't good to you."

"He's not good to any of us." Katie lifted her shoulders. "Logan! Get out here." She shouted, piercing my eardrums. "Boys are so dumb."

248

DEPENDING ON YOU

I smirked. "That's not very nice. Your brother is a good boy."

Katie rolled her eyes. "Yeah, okay."

Logan appeared and hit Katie in the back of the head. "You're so annoying."

"Logan, be nice to your sister. Have a seat, I want to talk to you guys." I straightened my posture making sure my cleansing breaths were going throughout my whole body.

"Mom and Dad are getting divorced." Katie pulled her leg under her.

"Katie." I lowered my head. "She's right. Your father and I are not good for each other and that's not good for you."

"About time." Logan leaned back and crossed his leg. "I was wondering how long you were going to let him get away with his crap."

"The stuff between your father and me isn't something for you to worry about. You can love us both the same. We'll just live in different houses, maybe in different states, but that shouldn't change the way you feel about either of us. This has nothing to do with either one of you."

"We're not children. We get it. Dad doesn't even try to hide the fact that he's sleeping with half the town. You're too good for him." Logan cracked his knuckles and stretched.

"Logan's right, for once." Katie tossed a pillow at her brother. "We're on your side, Mom."

"I'm not asking you to take sides. I only wanted you to know what's going on." I closed my eyes and blew out my breath. "There's more, and it might be hard to hear."

"Are you leaving Dad for Cate?" Logan raised his brow.

"No." I laughed. "It's not a bad idea, but that's not it."

249

JESSICA AIKEN-HALL

"It's okay with us if you've found someone else. We wouldn't blame you." Katie turned to face me.

"That's not it, either." I rubbed my eyes. "I've been keeping parts of myself hidden from people, even Cate didn't know until last week."

"Cate didn't know?" Katie sucked in air. "It must be bad."

"It's not bad. Well parts of it were, but that's behind me. When I was eighteen years old, I got pregnant. The circumstances don't matter, but let's say things were out of my control. I was scared and kept the pregnancy from everyone. I gave the baby up for adoption and..."

"Wait, so you're saying I have another sibling?" Katie pointed at Logan. "There's someone other than this numbskull that I share my DNA with?"

"Yes, you guys have a half-brother. His name is Silas and he's nineteen."

"That's so cool." Katie bounced in her seat. "Can we meet him?"

"Yes, of course. He lives in New York, so he's only a few hours away." I looked to see if I could read Logan's reaction. "What do you think? I know it's a lot to take in."

Logan nodded. "It's cool. It'd be nice to have an older brother, I guess."

"Are you sure? I'd understand if you were upset with me. I know it's a lot to digest."

"No, I'm fine. I don't understand why you couldn't have told us before." Logan picked at the frayed thread on his pant leg. "You make it a big deal for us not to lie to you, but you keep this huge thing from us."

"That's true. I do ask you not to lie to me. I didn't mean to keep this from you. There are other parts to the story that aren't

250

important, but it's what kept me from being able to tell anyone. I was scared. I'm sorry that I ask things of you that I couldn't do myself." I leaned my head back into the cushion. "I love you both very much. I never wanted to hurt you."

"It's fine, Mom. Logan doesn't understand how hard it must have been for you." Katie put her hand on mine. "It must have been so lonely to not even be able to share this with your best friend."

"I'm not mad. It's just a lot." Logan shrugged. "When can we meet him?"

"I'll have to call him and set it up." I smiled. "You know, he kind of looks like you."

Logan smirked. "So, you're saying he's hot?"

"Don't be gross." Katie rolled her eyes. "I can't wait to meet him."

"Thank you both for being so incredibly awesome. You make me so proud to be your mom."

"You're the reason we're so amazing." Katie batted her eyelashes. "We learned it from you."

"Come and give me a hug." I held my arms open and soaked in the love from my children who lingered between the last days of their childhood and the first days of their adulthood. "We're in this together. I'll always be here for you no matter what."

Chapter Forty-Four

PATTI

Silas waved as we pulled into his driveway. "Are you guys ready?" I asked as I put the car in park.

"Yeah." Katie jumped out of the backseat and rushed over to Silas, wrapping her arms around him.

"Thank god there's someone else who gets to deal with her." Logan shook his head. "He does look like me, doesn't he?"

"He does." I took his hand. "Let's go meet your big brother."

"Hi Patti." Silas had Katie's hand. "You must be Logan." He held his fist out.

Logan bumped his fist. "Hi."

"My mom is excited to meet you all. She made her famous chocolate chip cookies." Silas led the way into the two-story house.

"Hello, I'm Elaine." The older woman extended her hand. "I'm so glad you could make it."

With my hand in hers, she placed her other hand on top. "Thank you for welcoming us into your home."

"Don't be silly, you're always welcome here." She pointed to

DEPENDING ON YOU

the living room. "Why don't we go have some cookies and get to know each other?"

Silas nudged Katie in the side. "See, I told you."

They giggled as Logan trailed behind them. When we were settled into our seats, Mr. Hart joined us. "Hello. I'm glad you made it in one piece. Traffic can be a killer."

"We don't live too far away, so it wasn't too bad at all." I crossed my feet and perched on the edge of my seat.

"That's right, Silas told us that." Mr. Hart put his pipe in the corner of his mouth and lit a match. "Do you mind if I smoke?"

Elaine took the pipe out of his mouth. "I told you to smoke that thing outside." She placed it on the coffee table. "Excuse his poor manners."

"It's fine, really." I smiled.

"Nonsense. I hate when he smokes that thing anyway." Elaine sat on the chair across from me and picked up the tray of cookies. "Help yourself. They're my specialty."

"Mom." Silas covered his face. "Give them a chance to relax before you push the cookies."

Katie took one and bit into it. "Mmm, these are the best I've ever had."

Elaine held the tray in front of Logan. "Go on."

Logan took one. "Thank you, ma'am."

"You have such a beautiful home. Is this where you grew up?" I asked Silas.

"Yes, I've lived here all my life. It was cool living in the biggest house on the street. We had some killer pool parties, too." Silas crossed his leg over his knee.

"We always tried to fill this place with children and laughter. Silas always had a group of friends here with him." Elaine

253

folded her hands and set them in her lap. "You know, what you did for us is something I will never be able to repay you for. We tried for so many years to have a baby, but it wasn't meant to be. When we got the call about Silas our whole world got so much brighter."

"I'm so glad he had you for parents. I always worried about him and wondered how he was doing. Not a day went by that I didn't think about him." Nervousness made my foot tap on the hardwood floor.

"And I was always worried that you'd change your mind and take him back from us." Elaine placed her hand on her heart. "I loved him the second I met him. He has been my greatest joy."

"I am pretty awesome." Silas chuckled. "I did have a good life, and now it's even better because I have two moms and siblings. I begged Mom for a little brother for as long as I can remember."

"That's true, he did. When the adoption agency closed its doors, I didn't know where to turn. We were older parents, and I didn't want to go through the heartache of being turned down. We were happy with the family we had." Elaine watched Logan nibble his cookie. "Was it hard for you after you had your other children?"

I nodded. "It was never not hard. I didn't want to give Silas up, but I didn't have any options. I was on my own. I knew he deserved more than I could have given him. When I got pregnant with Logan, I cried every day."

"I'm sorry, I shouldn't have asked. It's none of my business." Elaine picked up a cookie and picked a piece off.

"No, it's okay. You can ask me anything. I owe you so much for taking such good care of him. I'm grateful that you are so welcoming. I know it must be hard for you." I pushed up a smile. "I don't want to take him away from you."

"I know that." Elaine brushed the crumbs off her lap. "He's part of you. It's important to me that he has a relationship with all three of you. I can tell you want what's best for him, and I know he'll do a terrific job as a big brother."

"I'm pretty excited about it, too." Silas clapped his hands. "I can't wait to see what happens next."

"It's going to be way less exciting than our first week together." I held my hand up. "I'm open to making new, happy memories though."

"I'd like that." Elaine's face lit up. "It feels so nice to finally have the house full. I hope you know you've officially become part of the family. You all have an open invitation here anytime."

"That's very generous." My body relaxed into my chair. "I'd never turn down expanding our family. I can't put into words how much this means to me. You've put some of my biggest fears to rest."

"Oh, honey, the only thing you should ever be afraid of is the time you waste when you should be living." Elaine handed Mr. Hart his pipe. "Looks like we have a reason to celebrate."

One
Year
Later

Chapter Forty-Five
PATTI

The last of the boxes were finally unpacked. I put my hands on my hips and looked around the house. "I can't believe I'm finally home."

"It's serendipity that this house was put on the market when you started looking." Cate put her hand around my waist.

"I'm so glad your dad saved my mom's furniture. Now I really feel like I'm home. I haven't felt like this since I moved away all those years ago." I leaned my head on Cate's shoulder.

"I'm so glad you're only a short walk from me again. I never thought I'd have you back in my life everyday again." Cate wiped her arm across her forehead. "I'm getting too old for this. You better stay put now."

"You'll have to wheel me out of here in a body bag." I laughed.

"My god Mom, that's gruesome." Katie turned up her nose and sat on the couch.

"Your mom always had a way with words." Cate smirked. "Lawrenceville Library won't know what to do with your talent."

258

DEPENDING ON YOU

"The first thing I'm going to do is update the romance section. Let's give the little old ladies of this town something to think about. They're old, not dead." I held my belly and snorted.

"Eww. That's gross." Katie held her hand up. "There's no way I'm telling anyone we're related."

"Looks like I'll be getting myself a library card." Cate doubled over in laughter. "Although I don't really need to read about that stuff now, if you know what I mean." She wiggled her eyebrows.

Katie stuck her finger in her mouth and gagged. "Is this what it's going to be like living with you two?"

"Oh, honey, this is only the beginning. We have twenty years of mischief and mayhem to make up for." I crossed my legs. "I think I'm going to wet myself."

"Be nice to your mom. You won't always be young and beautiful. You'll be an old lady like us someday." Cate patted Katie on the back.

"You two are crazy." Katie spread out on the couch. "I'm glad you're happy. Just keep the visuals to a minimum. I have virgin ears, remember?"

"And we're going to keep it that way, right?" I tapped my foot and crossed my arms.

"Not if you get all those nasty books." Katie rolled over and turned on her phone. "Just kidding. I'm going to stay pure until I find the right guy. There's no way I want to fall for someone like Dad. No offense, but he's a jerk."

"Good plan." Cate and I spoke at the same time.

"Why don't you two go have some tea and cookies or something?" Katie shooed us out of the living room. "I want to call my friends."

259

I sat on my bed and waited for Cate to join me. "Can you believe it's been over twenty years since we had a sleep over?"

"I know." Cate pulled her legs under her. "We should do it again."

"It feels so weird to be here without Mom. I miss her so much." I rubbed my hand on the mattress. "This will be my first night sleeping here without her."

"I'll stay." Cate took my hand. "She's still here, just in a different way."

"I still can't believe she knew Danny wasn't who I thought he was. How did she know? I didn't even know."

"She was good at seeing people for who they were. She loved you so much and she wanted the best for you." Cate smiled. "Her and Dad were such good friends. After you moved away, we spent so much time here with her. Sammy, too."

"When we'd talk on the phone, she'd tell me about everything you guys were up to. Thank you for sticking around when I couldn't. I wished she would have known about Silas. I know she would have loved him."

"She knows about him now." Cate got up and looked out the window. "And I know she loves him. She loved everyone. She was the best mom I ever met. Better than any TV mom."

"I'm glad you told her what happened. At least the part you knew. I hate that I made her think it was her I was trying to get away from. She didn't deserve that."

"She never thought that. She wanted the best for you, even if that meant you weren't home. She never said anything about being sad. She was happy." Cate closed the curtain. "Have you told Katie about the treehouse?"

"No way. I don't need her first summer in Lawrenceville

DEPENDING ON YOU

spent in the love shack." I laughed. "I think I want to bring Andrew out there."

"Really?" Cate raised her eyebrows. "Make sure you bring your phone with you in case one of you fall out of there."

"We're not that old." I put my hand on my hip. "But maybe you could help me get it fixed up."

"That's probably a good idea. I can't believe the steps held up all these years. I thought for sure Jake was going to break his hip." Cate giggled. "Don't you think it would be safe to rent a room somewhere?"

"No way. I built the love shack so we could use it. I think it's time. Don't you?" I threw a pillow at her.

"I don't know. We're almost forty. Do you really think we should be up in the air doing acrobats? At eighteen it made sense, now I see the emergency room in our future." Cate tossed the pillow back at me.

"We're only as old as we feel, and when I'm with you I feel like a kid again. The best years of our life are ahead of us." I joined Cate at the window. "Do you remember how many hours we spent out there? I think we should get a hot tub. That way we can nurse our sore muscles after we make up for lost time in the treehouse."

"As Katie would say... eww." Cate tossed her head back and laughed. "A hot tub sounds nice though. That could be the new love shack. The retirement version."

"Cate, we're not old. We're like wine, better with age. We've got to embrace the changes as they come. No more wasted time." With Cate's hand in mine, I lifted them up. "To new memories."

261

Chapter Forty-Six

CATE

I handed Sammy a paper bag sack. "Good luck on your first day."

"What's this?" Sammy opened the bag. "You made me lunch?" The smile spread across her face. "That's so nice of you."

"I'm proud of you. You've worked so hard to get to this point. I hope you love your new job." I kissed her cheek.

"I couldn't have done it without you. Knowing you're there has meant everything to me." Sammy rolled up the bag. "Who would have thought I'd ever work in a library?"

"Patti knows a good worker when she sees one." I picked up my bag and took out my keys. "I'm coming with you. I have a deadline I have to meet."

"It's pretty cool you're a journalist now. I know how bad you wanted this job." Sammy turned off the lights. "Even cooler you get to work with Jake."

"It is cool. Everything has a way of working out. I like to think Dad has something to do with how well things are going." I tossed my bag in the backseat.

262

DEPENDING ON YOU

"I think you're right." Sammy buckled her seatbelt. "When I was at rehab we had to come up with a vision for our future and make a list of the people we wanted to make proud. Most of the people on my list were dead, except you and Patti. I know what you gave up taking care of me when you didn't have to. I would have been screwed if you would have left. Thank you for everything you've done for me. You're more like my mom than my sister."

I put my hand over my heart. "Aww, Sammy, that means a lot to me. It wasn't easy, but I wouldn't have changed any of it. Sure, there were some things that could have been better, but then I don't know if I'd appreciate all that I have right now. Life is one big lesson we spend all our days figuring things out. If you're lucky everything will work out in the end."

"And if it doesn't work out, it's not the end." Sammy smiled. "I learned that in therapy. Don't give up, tomorrow is a better day."

"We've come a long way." I took her hand in mine. "I'm glad to have you by my side. Having a little sister's not that bad after all." Laughter filled the space between us.

"Hey." Sammy scowled before going back to cackling. "You're not too bad yourself."

"What do you have planned tonight?" I asked as I backed out of the driveway.

Sammy squirmed in her seat. "I have a date." She held up her hand. "I know what you're going to say..."

"What am I going to say?" I raised my brow. "Have fun?"

"I thought you'd be upset. I know I'm not that far into my recovery, but this guy is so nice." Sammy rolled down her window. "I want what you and Jake have."

"You deserve happiness. As long as you're happy and he's

263

good to you there's no reason for me to interfere. Shocker, I know." I turned the radio down. "I had my chance to make my mistakes, and no one stopped me. I'm not saying you're making a mistake, only that you need the chance to live. What's the point of life without risks?"

"I like this new improved, less uptight version of you." Sammy put her arm out the window. "Love looks good on you."

"I was never uptight." I narrowed my eyes. "Okay, maybe I was, but to be fair I was under a lot of stress. I hope you never have to live with a stick up your butt."

"You weren't that bad, but I'm glad you've relaxed." Sammy turned up the music. "You're still listening to this stuff? You know it's not the nineties anymore, right?"

"Too bad because that was the best decade. Everything was better in the nineties." I tapped my fingers on the steering wheel. "Listening to this CD brings me back to some of the best days of my life. Patti and I listened to these songs every time we were together. Kids your age have no idea what good music is."

"I'm not saying I don't like it. All I'm saying is that you're missing out on so much good stuff." Sammy moved her body to the beat.

I increased the volume. "This is my favorite." Sammy and I sung with Tracy Chapman to *Fast Car* until we arrived at the library. Jake and Patti were outside on the steps drinking coffee.

"Looks like a job I can handle." Sammy laughed.

"Maybe they're waiting for you to welcome you on your first day." I shrugged. "It is a nice morning. Why not spend it in the sunshine?"

"A job with windows and coffee? I don't think it gets any

better than that." Sammy took her lunch and joined Patti and Jake.

Jake handed me a cup. "I thought you could use this. I know you have a deadline to meet."

"Thanks. Lucky for me I know the librarian so I can probably sneak this in." I took a sip of the hot liquid. "You remembered how I like it."

Jake nodded. "Of course." He twisted his dress shoe into the concrete step. "So, Patti and I were talking. How do you feel about a double date? We can go get some dinner and maybe even recreate the prom."

I lifted my eyebrows. "She didn't happen to mention the love shack, did she?"

Jake lifted his shoulder and grinned. "I don't know what you're talking about."

I covered my face. "I don't know why she's so insistent on using that dilapidated treehouse."

"I think it sounds romantic, but if you don't want to, I understand." Jake took a drink. "I've got to run. I have a meeting with a bookstore."

"I'm so happy you moved back to Lawrenceville. I'm sure selling books isn't as exciting as your old job, but at least we get to work together."

"It's not so bad." Jake bent down and kissed me. "And who knows when I'll be selling your book."

"I'd have to write it first." I pushed the hair out of my face.

"Then what are you waiting for?" Jake winked. "You made my dreams come true, now it's time for yours."

265

Chapter Forty-Seven

PATTI

"You look so beautiful, Cate." I looked at our reflection in the mirror. "Jake is going to lose his mind."

"And so is Andrew." Cate put her arm around me. "We look even better than we did the first time."

"You think?" I raised my brow. "We're old ladies now."

"We're mature. And now we know what we want out of life." Cate applied her mascara. "How cool is it that we ended up with the same guys we were in love with in high school?"

"It's been a long road to get here." I grabbed my shawl. "I want to show you something before the guys get here. Come with me."

"Where are we going?" Cate set her makeup down and reached for her sweater.

"You'll see." I held out my hand and led her outside. "Get in the car."

"At least you're not taking me to the treehouse." Cate giggled.

DEPENDING ON YOU

"That's later." I turned the radio on. "I made myself a playlist with all of our favorites."

"Playlists? Ugh. CDs are where it's at." Cate smirked. "It does sound great though."

"Yeah, and no skipping." I moved my head to the music. "I have a whole list of just Tom Petty. I hit shuffle and let his voice whisk me away."

"How is that different than a CD?" Cate wiggled in her seat to the song.

"It's not, I guess, except I can have every song on my phone and a CD only holds like twelve." I pulled my car into the cemetery.

"What are you doing? Are you really trying to recreate prom night?" Cate held onto her seat.

"No, we're in control of how tonight goes. I want to show you something." I reached for her hand.

"I'd be lying if I didn't tell you I'm a little anxious." Cate fidgeted in her seat.

"Relax, everything is going to be alright." As I pulled up to the knoll, Jake and Andrew were waiting for us. "See, I told you we're safe."

"What are they doing here?" Cate unbuckled her seatbelt and leaned forward.

"We're going to start the night here. We have something to celebrate." I took the keys out of the ignition. "Come with me."

Jake and Andrew stood side by side with matching smiles on their faces. "You ladies look amazing." Andrew straightened his tie.

I locked arms with Cate and led her to the guys. "I wanted to start the celebration here because we need to reclaim what was ours.

267

This place brought us both so much comfort when we needed it most. When I came here seeking comfort it led to the worst night of our lives. I wanted to do something to bring that comfort back so we have a place we can go when life gets overwhelming."

Jake and Andrew stepped to the side.

"What is this?" Cate tilted her head.

"I know when we were kids, we wanted to buy this land and build a house on it. The quietest neighbors around." I held my hand out and pointed in front of us. "They wouldn't let me buy the land, but I was still able to buy us our house."

Cate covered her mouth. "You didn't."

"I did. This is our stone. Our plot. If you want to spend eternity with me, this is the place." I put my hand on the house shaped slab of granite.

Cate kneeled down and traced her fingers over the letters. "Cate Silver and Patti Thomas best friends forever."

"Check out the back." I helped her to her feet.

"Depending on you." Cate wiped a tear off her cheek. "This is beautiful, Patti."

"And this bench so we can come enjoy our house on the hill." I sat on the decorative stone. "Friends forever."

"Friends forever." Cate joined me on the bench and put her arm around me. "This is the best gift I've ever received."

Jake popped the cork on the champagne. "And here's to the weirdest housewarming party I've ever been to."

Cate pulled me close. "But look at that view." We admired the town I had run from for the past twenty years. It was finally home again. Filled with friends and love that had always been here, waiting for me.

Thank you for reading Depending On You

I hope you enjoyed it. If you did, you can help others find this book by leaving a review. As an independent author hearing what readers think is so important. It helps us in so many ways. I'd be honored to hear what you thought!

Consider leaving a REVIEW here

You can also sign up for my newsletter , so you can find out about the next book as soon as it is available. You'll also get a free gift when you sign up!

You can also follow me on Facebook or visit my website, https://www.jessicaaikenhall.com.

Acknowledgments

Thank you to my family for allowing me the time and space to create these stories.

Thank you to my best friend, Heather, for giving me inspiration for this novel from the adventures of our youth.

Many thanks to the people who helped bring Depending On You to life.

Shower of Schmidt Designs for the beautiful cover.

Proofreading By the Page for editing and polishing my words.

Debbie Russell and Michele Avery for beta reading.

To the Coffee Queens: Thank you for your support, encouragement and push to keep writing. You have all helped me so much with your friendship and kindness.

Thank you to the readers. Without you, my characters would never have any fun! Your honest feedback is always appreciated and helps improve my craft. Reviews help other readers as much as they help me. Please consider leaving one.

About the Author

Jessica Aiken-Hall, author of her award-winning memoir, *The Monster That Ate My Mommy* lives in New Hampshire with her husband, three children, and three dogs. She is a survivor of child abuse and domestic violence and is a fierce advocate. Her mission is to help others share their story.

She has a master's degree in Mental Health Counseling, with over a decade of experience as a social worker. She is also a Reiki Master and focuses her attention on healing.

When she is not writing, she enjoys listening to Tom Petty, walking along the beach, looking at the moon, and watching murder shows.

To follow what she's doing next check out http://www.jessicaaikenhall.com.

CPSIA information can be obtained
at www.ICGtesting.com
Printed in the USA
BVHW071925150222
629100BV00003B/25